WILDCAT

TIMBER-GHOST, MONTANA CHAPTER

DEVIL'S HANDMAIDENS MC
BOOK 7

D.M. EARL

© Copyright 2024 D.M. Earl
All rights reserved.
Cover by Drue Hoffman, Buoni Amici Press
Editing by Karen Hrdlicka
Proofread by Joanne Thompson

All rights reserved. No part of this book may be reproduced in any form or by any electronic or mechanical means, including information storage and retrieval systems—except in the case of brief quotations embodied in critical articles or reviews—without permission in writing from the author.

This book is a work of fiction. The names, characters, and places portrayed in this book are entirely products of the author's imagination or used fictitiously. Any resemblance to actual events, locales, or persons, living or dead, is entirely coincidental and not intended by the author.

The unauthorized reproduction or distribution of this copyrighted work is illegal. Criminal copyright infringement, including infringement without monetary gain, is investigated by the FBI and is punishable by up to five years in federal prison and a fine of $250,000.

If you find any eBooks being sold or shared illegally, please contact the author at dm@dmearl.com.

ACKNOWLEDGMENTS

Karen Hrdlicka and **Joanne Thompson** my editing and proofreading team. I'm totally blessed to be working with these two ladies. Between them Karen and Joanne polish my stories so they shine. With their eyes on my stories I feel y'all are getting the best book possible due to their experience and knowledge of how I write.

Debra Presley and **Drue Hoffman** @ **Buoni Amici Press**. These two women are the BOMB. My two publicists work endlessly to handle the social media aspect, formatting, publishing and so much more which then allows me to concentrate on my writing. With them as part of the team I know everything is getting done and correctly and timely.

Enticing Journey Promotions. Ena helps me with every new release and are very professional and always on top of everything.

Bloggers. To every single one of you. What you do for each and every one of my releases and stories is something that I can never repay. Please know how much I appreciate each share, mention, post, and video.

My **DM's Babes** (ARC Team) and **DM's Horde** (Reader's group). These women in these two groups have become part of my chosen family. I'm thrilled to spend time and engage with each and every one of them.

READERS without each of Y'all I'd not be able to live out my life's dream of writing books that make people tingle and just feel deep in their souls. Your support fills my heart and feeds my soul.

Chuck. Without you and your support not sure I'd have written as much as I have. Thank you for always having my back and supporting me. Means the world babe. Luv ya.

ONE
'WILDCAT'
FRANKIE

My God, my club sisters are dropping like damn flies. Never thought I'd see the women I admire and call sisters, and more importantly my *chosen family*, be able to not only manage but also find men who fit their personalities to a T.

These are the thoughts running through my mind as I've just watched Raven say her I dos to her high school sweetheart, Ash. Never would I have thought our hilarious technology nerd would have fallen for a Montana cowboy, though it makes sense. Raven grew up in Timber-Ghost and her entire family is now right back here in town, well, all around it. Watching them exchange their vows and kiss, it brings back memories I've tried to keep at the back of my mind. Fuck, don't need that shit to surface now, our club has had enough drama to last us all for the rest of our lives. Damn, between Tink, Shadow, Taz, Vixen, Glory, and now Raven, we need a damn break. Or a vacation. Yeah, maybe for the entire club, though that will never happen, there's too many bad people out there inflicting pain on innocents. Seems like I keep picking occupations to try and save people, though this one doesn't have as many rules as my last as a cop.

Hearing everyone clapping, I put my hands together to join the crowd as we celebrate our friend's happy day, which she deserves totally. I mean, she almost died not too long ago because of Ash's asshole father. Moving away from that dark shit on such a beautiful day, I look around and can't believe how we've become such a close-knit community, because at one time no one wanted the Devil's Handmaidens Motorcycle Club anywhere near Timber-Ghost. Over the years, Tink and our club have proven ourselves to the townsfolk. As we all make our way to take a few pictures, I feel someone plow into me from the back. When I turn around, our enforcer has a shit-eating grin on her face. And my God, to see her in a dress blows my damn mind. *Shadow is in a dress*, I think to myself yet again. Maybe I should pinch myself. And to top it off, there's no blood, brains, or other body matter dripping down the front of her.

"So, you up next there, Wildcat? Let's see if you can live up to your club's name. Some dude would be lucky to have you, sister. Though I haven't seen any wildcat in you lately, or actually ever. Who gave you that name?"

Laughing, I ignore her comment or dig, however I look at it. Little does she know; been there done that. Just that brief thought brings an overwhelming sadness to my heart. I can't change my decisions, even if I wanted to. Life goes on and, unfortunately for me, mine is moving along in Montana and not New York. I do reach out to my family occasionally, though I make sure they have no idea where I'm at. That can't be shared, or I'll be bringing a shit ton of trouble to our neck of the woods. Both good and bad. Especially if my location gets out to Malcolm, he'll lose his ever-loving mind. And I don't want to add any more pain or sorrow to him. I'd done enough the day I walked away, though it was because he pushed me away for good.

Today has been a great day and also a day of hard to remember memories for me. Thank God I have one of the cabins behind Tink's huge ranch home, because tonight I need some quiet and alone time. After I remove my colorful dress and shoes, I change into some comfortable lounge clothes. Once settled, I grab a huge bottle of water since I did some drinking at the reception held here at the ranch. And got to say, Heartbreaker did a phenomenal job with planning and pulling it all together. It was beyond breathtaking with all those wildflowers everywhere, well, because those are what Raven adores and Ash adores her, so he made sure wherever you looked there were wildflowers.

I walk to the bedroom, open the closet, and move stuff around to grab the Rubbermaid that holds my entire life before the Devil's Handmaidens. I drag it to the couch and sit down, pulling the lid off. The memories hit me so hard I have to lean back and take a few breaths. Damn, maybe tonight isn't the right time to go through all this stuff. Last time I spoke to my mom, she told me everyone was doing well and seemed happy. That was all I ever wanted for everyone back home. Taking a deep breath, I lean forward and start to pull shit out and place it on the table in front of the couch. When everything is out, I push the bin over and start to go through it slowly. Pictures of my parents and siblings bring a few tears to my eyes. I gulp some water down as the pictures start to show me growing up, and the first one with both Malcolm and me in it has my eyes let loose. It was our freshman dance and the first one we'd ever gone to, but definitely not our last.

Looking at his handsome face never gets old. Even though he was young, he was always a big kid. By freshman year he was well over six feet tall and would grow another couple of inches before he reached his adult height. His caramel skin was beyond gorgeous, especially with his multifaceted eye color. They were a mix of gray, green, and blue. Depending on what he wore, his eye color changed.

Moving stuff around, I see a couple of the pictures I want and grab them. Leaning back with the photos in one hand and my water bottle in the other, I drink more water before replacing the cap and putting it on the table and then getting cozy on the couch. I start to go through the small stack of pictures as memories flood my brain like an old-time picture show. My God, we were so young and naïve. Each dance photo shows how fast we were growing up but the look in both of our eyes never changed. Well, it did, we fell more and more in love. That love went from a child's love to best friend love and finally to an adult one. When Malcolm went down on a knee while I was in my last year of college, my entire family was in on it.

We were doing our usual morning routine of jogging through Central Park. As we turned to head back to our apartment, Malcolm came to an abrupt stop by one of the waterfalls and grabbed my hands. Both of us were sweating and kind of out of breath, I didn't know if something was wrong with him or not. Then I heard the music coming toward us. When I turned, both of our families were making their way to us, my baby brother with his iPad and speaker in his hands. The song "At Last" by Etta James was playing and it sent shivers down my spine. When I turned back to my man, he was on one knee in front of me, a jewelry box in his hand. My eyes literally popped outta my head. We talked about this and wanted to wait until I finished college with my Bachelor of Science in Criminal Justice Administration and Malcolm finish medical school and got settled into his residence program. His beautiful gray blue-green eyes were glittering as they looked right into my grayish hazel eyes. This had been my dream ever since we first met and even though it was before I thought he'd ask; my heart was pounding as my mind started to see our dream of the future together.

When Malcolm asked, I didn't even let him finish, I jumped him as our families all laughed and cheered. The ring was perfect: it was a diamond solitaire with our birthstones on either side. So, on the left was an opal for my October birthday and on the right was a peridot to match Malcolm's August birthday. The band was thick so none of the stones stood out. He thought of everything because he knew I'd never want to take the ring off and if, no when, I became a cop, couldn't have a huge stone sticking out of the setting.

The next ten months went by in a blur. I planned with my mom, sisters, and Malcolm's mom, aunt, and sister. Everything was so easy, it just amazed all of us. In the meantime, I graduated summa cum laude from college with my degree and immediately was accepted into the police academy—which I flew through—and started my career at the police station as a patrol office with a senior officer alongside of me. Malcolm was headed off to medical school, which meant our time was going to be very limited. So, we decided to take a short trip to Bear Mountain State Park, one of our favorite places to go to relax and unwind. Both of our parents surprised us with a really nice cabin rental. So off we went, naïve and stupid as fuck. Two young adults off for a short week away before their lives went crazy. Little did we know how that short trip would change our lives forever.

The cabin was quaint and rustic but gorgeous. It had everything we needed. One bedroom and bath, with a small kitchenette and a quaint living room. Outside was a front porch with a barbecue and farther out a firepit overlooking a body of water down the mountain from where we were staying. The next cabin was at least a half-acre or more away and not even sure it was rented at the time we were there. The first couple of days were beyond fabulous. We hiked, swam, and just spent quality time together. On the third or fourth morning, can't recall which, we were sitting on the front porch when two male hikers approached, calling out a greeting.

Malcolm immediately was his friendly self but something about the two men was off to me. My cop training had me casually walk back into our cabin and I grabbed the small handgun my dad always told me to carry, no matter what. This was an argument Malcolm and I had. He hated guns and didn't want me to carry, which was asinine and plum crazy. I was on the fast track to becoming not only a cop but hopefully one day a detective, for God's sake. I also grabbed my mace, putting that in my pocket of my jacket. Then took the gun and put it in the holster in the back of my jeans.

I made my way back outside and the two men were now sitting on the stairs in the front of the cabin. Malcolm looked my way, and I could see his concern about these unexpected visitors, who seemed to be making themselves comfortable. They started to ask some personal questions, like if we were out there alone and if we had a few bucks we could loan them. Malcolm came closer to me and told them our parents had run to get some groceries but would be back shortly, and we were expecting more of our family to arrive later in the day. They looked at each other before their eyes shifted back at us. The look they gave us was not only dangerous but filled with so much evil we both felt it. I knew they were going to try and change the path our lives were on. And I'd fight to make sure they didn't. Or that was my thoughts.

Malcolm took a chance, pushing me back into the cabin and telling me to lock the door. I could hear the struggle outside as I grabbed first my cell phone and then the satellite phone Malcolm's dad insisted we take with. The cell had no reception, but the satellite immediately started up and I dialed 911. When the call connected, I calmly told the operator in a whispered voice our names and what was going on and where we were. She told me to stay on the line as she called the park's rangers. She also put out an emergency call to any available law enforcement officers close to the park. I told her I was also a cop, though new. Just as I started to give a description, I heard Malcolm scream out in pain.

"Frankie, stay inside where you are safe. I know it's hard but going out there puts not only your fiancé in more danger but also yourself. Stay put. Please listen to me, I know what I'm talking about."

"I can't, he sounds like he's in a lot of pain and I can't just stand around. I'll put the satellite phone in the back of the bookcase so you can listen in as much as you can. Will leave the door open too. Thank you for all you've done and for trying to help us."

"No, damn it, Frankie, don't go out there. Come on, stay and talk with me. It won't be long; backup is on its way."

Once again, I whispered a thank you then I hid the phone with its open line so she could hear what transpired. With the gun in my hand and the mace in my pocket, I made my way to the window first. What I saw I'll never forget. The two men were trying to hang a half-naked Malcolm off a tree by the edge of the mountain. He was fighting like crazy, though I could see he was already injured by the amount of blood on him. And where the blood was coming from explained why his pants were hanging around his ankles. That pissed me off, so I took a deep breath or two before I opened the door slowly, though not as quietly as I hoped because it slipped my mind how loud the hinges were. They needed some WD40, which we were joking about before our unwelcome guests showed up.

"Step away from him now, you motherfucking cocksuckers. I said, let him go! Now, before I blow both of your damn heads off."

First one then the other guy turned as they glared my way. That's when I heard the words that would change my life.

"No, Frankie, go back in. There's more than these two asswipes. Watch out, check your six. Don't worry about me, protect yourself, get back in the cabin."

I heard him before I saw him. When I went to turn around, off to my right he appeared. I shifted then aimed in that direction, so when a huge man came barreling toward me, I pulled the trigger, hitting him center mass. He immediately fell backward hard onto the ground off the deck. I could hear boots hitting the ground as I turned and before I could think about getting another shot off, one of the assholes seemed to stagger before he was right in front of me. He swung and managed to hit the gun from my hand. The gun went flying as he tackled me back through the cabin door. His weight sent me to the floor and I immediately lost my breath. By the time I could think, I had banged my head hard on the wooden floor. Looking at the one who manhandled me, I saw another guy was also inside. He slammed the door hard as he stomped toward me.

"Bitch, you're gonna pay plenty for what you just did to Buck. He's got kids, you stupid cop whore."

As I thought to myself, *how did they know I was a cop*, the first punch took me by surprise. By the seventh or eighth I prayed I'd pass out before they took their party to the next level. Right before my mind went dark and blank, I heard my clothes being ripped from my body. The last thought before I lost consciousness, I prayed Malcolm was okay and still breathing.

Wiping my face, I reach for my water as I've had enough reminiscing for one night. Finishing off the pile, I move through them quickly. Then when finished, I push the photos to the side on the table. I stand up then walk to the kitchen. I open the refrigerator and grab the open bottle of wine. Opening the cabinet off to the side, I pull a wine glass out and fill it right to the top. I sit at the kitchen table and suck back my wine until my hands stop shaking. Not sure why, I pull my phone out and look up contacts. When I see his name, I hit the number and wait. When the voicemail kicks in, I listen to his deep, sexy voice. It hits me in my core, which is a reaction I've not experienced this deeply in a very long time. Well, since Malcolm and I were last together.

"Hi, you reached Mal. I'm not available so at the tone leave your name, number, and whatcha want or need. I'll try to get back to you as soon as I can. And, Frankie, if this is you, hear me, nothing has changed. Please get in touch with me. None of what happened was your fault. I miss your face, Beautiful. Damn it, I was wrong to push you away. Please, Frankie talk to me."

The beep sounds and I look at my cell then hit disconnect. I finish my glass of wine. Immediately I grab the bottle, chugging the rest of it, then lose it, sobbing at the table like I lost my best friend because I did. That life I dreamed about and wanted so bad is gone to me forever.

TWO
'WILDCAT'
FRANKIE

If that alarm goes off one more time, it's getting tossed right out the window. Right now I don't give a flying fuck if it's still closed up tightly. That's the huge bummer when you get loaded the night before because it makes it that much harder to get one's ass, well their entire body, out of bed. I turn to my left side, one hand under my head, the other curled up between my breasts. It's not even cold out but I'm starting to shiver. Fuck, what a way to wake up. The days of me doing this kind of drunken shit have gotten less, but every once in a while, I make sure to shove my own head up into my ass so I can relive what happened in the woods on that night.

I'm so up into my own thoughts, I literally jump when I hear pounding at my door. Shit, did I forget a meeting or something? No one, and I mean no one, usually wanders down to my cabin as it's out of the way, almost remote. Well, not totally true, as Avalanche has been here but not sure if it was his idea or mine. We are so much alike; damaged souls beyond repair. Grabbing my extra-large sweatshirt, I push my feet into my plush slippers and shuffle my way to the door. Since I don't see anyone, I turn to go back to bed, when again someone is pounding at the door.

"Who the hell's there and what do you want?"

"Open the door, Wildcat, it's Squirt. I need your help, please. Not sure what to do."

Knowing this isn't going to be a one and done with Hannah, shit, I mean Squirt and her drama, I let out a sigh. Love my little Devil's Handmaiden sister but she can be a total pain in the ass. I reach the entry, unlock the three locks, and open the door.

"Damn, Wildcat, what is this, Fort Knox? Didn't realize you had such valuable stuff in here."

I just roll my eyes as I wave her in. Thank God she has two travel coffee mugs in her hands since I've not even started my day.

"Sister, take a seat give me five minutes to start my day properly. Be right back."

With that, I head to the bathroom to take a pee, brush my teeth, and run a comb through my short curls, which then has me grabbing my spray bottle of water to calm them down. I open the medicine cabinet to grab my morning pills, which I wash down with a glass of water. No one wants to be around me without my meds for depression, anxiety, and PTSD. Not many of my sisters know I take them, but I did share with Tink, Glory, and Shadow. Oh, and Kiwi since I had that panic attack at The Wooden Spirits Bar & Grill, which is owned by our club. Since I manage it and Kiwi is my bartender and backup short-order cook, she was there and watched me fall apart one early morning not too long ago. So naturally I had to share and give her an explanation, as she was ready to call in all our sisters from the club. I am not a very open woman, so sharing with her brought up even more memories. *So this last month has really sucked balls, nope, ovaries* I think to myself, but that's my life. Could be worse, and I know I tend to try and let nothing keep me down.

Opening the bathroom door, I make my way into the kitchen/living room to find Squirt curled up on my sectional, looking at her phone, tears in her eyes. Oh shit, what drama are we having today?

"Okay, Squirt, what's going on that has you about to burst into tears? And not that I don't want to help, but my door isn't usually the first one you come to. Where are Tink and Shadow?"

She lifts her head and I swear she's the spitting image of our prez, Tink. *It's eerie,* I sometimes think to myself. Keeping my eye on her, I grab the travel mug and take a sip. Damn, that's some good stuff, must be from Tink's house. She doesn't splurge much but coffee is one of hers.

"Wildcat, if I'm bothering you then I'll go. And I came to you because I trust you and know you're a former cop, right? No, don't get your curls bouncing, it's a fact that we all know, though you aren't one to share anything with us. You of all people know there are no secrets in the Devil's Handmaidens. These women gossip like little old ladies in a nursing home, for Christ's sake. So I've got a problem and not sure how to handle it. And it kind of involves you, I think. First off, I'm almost positive, but is your legal name Frankie Comano? Well, shit, guess I'm on the right path by the look of sheer panic on your face. Hey, sister, breathe. Wildcat, come on, please breathe."

Struggling just hearing my name, I sit next to Squirt, placing my travel mug on the coffee table in front of us. Taking a moment, I put my head between my legs and try to recall what the therapist at the Blue Sky Sanctuary told me about how to breathe when I'm panicking. When Squirt starts to gently rub up and down my back, I start to relax. In… then… out and repeat. After a few minutes, I sit up and lean back into the couch as she pulls her hand away.

"Squirt, I know we know each other's given names, but not sure why you'd remember it, as I don't use it ever up here. What's up?"

"Well, I was in town at the bakery. Was thinking maybe I'd bring some treats for our chapel meeting this afternoon. There was a line, as usual. When the next number got pulled, I heard a guy after he ordered an Americano coffee ask if they knew a Frankie Camano, and if so, did they know where he could find her. I thought he said you were a friend of his little sister and he was in the area. Anyway, as most of the businesses in Timber-Ghost know not to talk about the club members, both of the women promptly told him they never heard that name, but if it was important to maybe go talk to

Sheriff George, as he knows just about everyone. I was watching him and when they mentioned the sheriff, he acted strange. So me being me, I pulled my phone out, took a chance, and snapped a couple of photos of him. They might not be the best but something about him seemed strange, and my gut told me he's not right or that he was lying. I thought maybe if I showed them to you, there's a chance he might be someone you know, or maybe not. I don't know, Wildcat, but Auntie Zoey—hush, don't tell her I called her that instead of Shadow—she always tells me to follow my gut, and that's what I did. Sorry if I upset you though, not my intention at all. I'm trying to have your back. Do you want to see the photo?"

I can feel my heart pounding in my chest as an instant headache starts between my eyes. My hands start to tremble, that's how scared I am the past has finally found me. No one in my family knows I'm living in Timber-Ghost, Montana, so why would some stranger be spouting off my name? Taking in a deep breath, I look at Squirt.

"First off, you, little sister, you didn't do anything wrong. I'm glad you're learning to follow your gut. You of all the prospects know how important that is. Now, the reason I'm freaking the fuck out is, and not many know this, but no one not even my family knows exactly where I'm living. So for someone to be looking for me, using my given name, has the hair on the back of my neck standing up. To be honest with you, Squirt, I ran from my prior life for a very specific reason: to protect those I love. If somehow the assholes found me, then not only me but our club has a problem, so let me see the picture you took. Thanks, Squirt, for having my back, means a lot."

She gives me a slight grin then reaches for her phone. She unlocks it then guess she's looking in her gallery for the photo. When she clicks on something then hands it to me, I close my eyes for a brief second, praying to all or anything that will listen this is going to be nothing. I open my eyes, lift the phone, and look down. And at that moment, my life changes forever.

One minute my eyes are staring at a face I never thought I'd ever have to see ever again, and the next second I'm curled up on the floor. Not even ten minutes later, after a call from Squirt, I hear the knock before the door flies open and Tink, Noodles, Heartbreaker, and Presley rush in. Presley grabs Squirt close as she's softly crying, and that's on me. She didn't know what to do so she put out the emergency call to our prez. Tink is the first to me as she kneels next to me, not saying a word, just running her hands through my short hair and down my back. Noodles pulls the table away so Heartbreaker can take a seat next to me. She must have given Tink a look because once my prez removes her hand from my hair, Heartbreaker pulls my head to her lap and she takes over rubbing my scalp.

Between the two of them and their kindness, I can't

control the first tear to fall down my face, but when followed by uncontrollable sobs, I hear a noise then Squirt is lying next to me, pulling me close. It is like a Devil's Handmaidens mosh pit between the four of us. Not sure how long we stay like this but then another loud racket can be heard before again the door flies open. This time it's Glory and two very pregnant sisters, Taz with Vixen.

One of the downfalls is most of the Devil's Handmaidens sisters all live on the property in the main house, cabins or in homes close by. Some within spitting distance. Though today I so appreciate the closeness. Before a word is said, Glory gets down on the floor while Taz and Vixen step over all of us and plop down on the couch above us. What surprises me is how they all know right now I don't want to talk about it. Their support is what is helping me to keep it together. Tink is rubbing my back, Heartbreaker is massaging my scalp, Squirt is spooning with me, and Glory puts her hands to my forehead. The constant contact is what keeps me in the present because my mind wants to travel down that dark motherfucking road I've spent the last couple of years avoiding.

First, you hear a distant sound like a truck or something roaring down the road to the cabins. Then doors slamming and finally something that sounds like wild animals in chase. The door is open, so when feet hit the front deck, we all look that way just as Shadow runs through it. Her eyes are crazy as fuck, the ice-blue literally glowing. She takes one look at all of us and lets out an animalistic growl to end all growls. She stomps toward us then squats down. Yeah, only she can pull that off, I'd fall right on my ass. Then she asks the million-dollar question.

"Wildcat, sister, whatcha need? Who am I skinning alive then strangling with their own intestines? Or I can bleed them like a chicken or tar and feather them. You tell me what you want and, sister, I'm there."

It takes maybe a minute, if that, before I hear Taz snort, Vixen fake coughs to hide her giggles, and Glory mutters under her breath "Ohhh fuck here we go again." I feel Squirt's shoulders shaking because she's laughing into my body. It's Tink, as always, who has that relationship with our enforcer and loudly, with so much emotion in her voice more tears fall down my cheeks, scolds.

"Damn it, Zoey, why do you always resort to violence, for Christ's sake? Can't you see we're having a moment trying to support Wildcat? Can't you be quiet for a second or two? Geez."

I've tilted to get a better view of Shadow and now she's glaring at our prez. Then she leans back, plops down on her butt, and raises her knees to lean her elbows on them. Never taking her eyes from Tink, she gives it right back.

"Goldilocks, how much time do you need? I've got all day."

With that, we all break out laughing as I watch Shadow's eyes turn to me. I can see her worry and concern so I give her a small smile, which she just nods to then looks at Tink and sticks her tongue out. Perfect. Just what I needed to get my head out of my ass. Then I hear something above me, which has all of us on the floor looking up. Doesn't take long for the smell to start to make its way around the room. Holy shit, one of the pregnant ones farted. Leave it to Shadow to be blunt and direct.

"Well, fuck, hope whoever dealt that deadly one didn't shat their bloomers. For God's sake, that is killer. Gotta get some air." One by one we get up and head outside. The last ones out are Taz and Vixen, giggling together, like they don't have a care in the world.

Guess it's time to figure out my next steps with these wonderful women who would and have dropped everything to have my back.

THREE
'MALCOLM'
MALTY

I've dreamt of this day for the last couple of years because I couldn't forget that face, those eyes, and that sick demented voice. Didn't think I'd be in the emergency room getting ready to enter a treatment room when said voice stopped me dead in my tracks. No way, it can't be. Not here in my safe place. I mean, what are the chances? The information I was given was there was an altercation in the federal prison, and they were transferring an inmate who was severely injured. Not sure about that, as from what I'm hearing that prisoner is running his mouth off pretty good for being in serious condition. I know my interns are waiting for me to enter the area, but not sure it's such a great idea. Am I able to treat this person as they should be treated, or will I do him more harm than good? I can't truthfully answer that question now. I quietly tell the two interns to go in and stay away from the patient. Then I turn and walk to the office of the emergency department and find my boss sitting at her desk. She looks up when I enter and close the door. Judy raises her eyebrow, which I'm seriously jealous of because I can't do that shit. I've tried, which is pitiful to even admit.

"There's an inmate who was just brought in. Not one-hundred-percent sure, but it sounds exactly like one of the men who attacked Frankie and me years ago. Not sure I can be his attending and treat him accordingly. I know we are shorthanded but, Judy, I'm being truthful. What do you want me to do?"

She knows my story, as I told it to her about a year ago. I have my moments and, thank God, today isn't one of them. At times I have to use a cane, not that often, but it happens. She asked and I told her the entire story. After all she's done for me, I owed it to her.

"Mal, grab the next patient. I'll handle this one. Did they give you any details or am I going to walk in blind?"

As we walk toward the treatment room, we can both hear his bellowing about suing us for not treating him like other patients because he's a prisoner. Judy just shakes her head as she pulls one of the portable iPads from the nurses' station. I watch her fling back the curtain and introduce herself. He starts saying sexual things to her and she replies with a, "Shut it or else."

I think she shocked him because for maybe fifteen seconds he's quiet, then all hell breaks loose. I can hear loud noises then an "oof" from I'm thinking one of the interns. Judy yells for security. I move toward the room, looking for something to use as a weapon. When I spot the toolbox, I reach inside, pulling out a large wrench.

Quietly I enter the room, and it's total chaos. The prisoner has one intern on the ground bleeding while he's trying to strangle the other with his hands cuffed. Not sure where the prison guard is but Judy is in the med drawer, which I'm sure she's looking for something to knock his ass out. Well, I have just the thing. As I approach, not sure, must have made a sound because he turns and that's the first look I get of one of the men who changed my life. Before I can do a thing, he smirks.

"You've got to be shittin' me. After all this time, I finally get eyes on you, *Malcolm*. Looks like you recovered, though wish we could have watched you hang from that tree, motherfucker. Would have if your bitch of a woman would have minded her own goddamn business, though we showed her who's boss, who wears the pants, didn't we? Then we showed you who was, ugh...."

Before he could spout any more of his filthy nastiness, I swing and hit him with the wrench hard. He goes down grabbing his center, groaning then squealing like a baby. Judy rushes around me and sticks him in the arm with a needle, and within seconds it's quiet once more. When she looks around to me, she mouths "Sorry." I just shrug. I don't care if people find out what all these bastards did to me. My biggest concern is if this one was in prison for most of the time since our attack, I can only pray the other guy is incarcerated too or maybe, fingers crossed, he's dead. Because if he isn't, then that means my Frankie isn't safe and, at the moment, I have no idea where the hell she is. That thought is what has me worried to death.

* * *

After my shift, I go immediately home to my townhouse to relax. That is after I get settled and feed my two dogs and three cats that are my roommates. Oh, who am I kidding? They're my fur babies. I go into the walk-in closet in my guest bedroom and pull out two Rubbermaids. Rummaging for what I am looking for, I pull out the phone book. I go through it until I find the number I am searching for. Over the years, we've reached out periodically. Mainly on the anniversary of our attack and when they would call to wish me happy birthday. There was kind of an unstated agreement of not talking or even mentioning Frankie. Not the way I wanted to play it, but not only do I love her parents, I respect their wishes. Her dad, Enzo, finally broke down one day and said they speak to their daughter a few times a month. Just knowing that gives me a little peace of mind, though not much. I want to talk to her too, but not happening anytime soon, obviously.

Knowing this call is going to bring up all the bullshit of our mixed past, I feel bad but need to make sure Frankie's okay. So I dial their number and wait. One ring then two. Before the third one the call engages and I hear a kid's voice.

"Hello, Camano house. Who's calling?"

The little voice brings a smile to my face when in the background an older kid's voice yells something about it being a residence not a house. Then footsteps and a grown man's voice is on the other end.

"Hi. Sorry 'bout that, the lil' one is quick. You got Enzo."

I clear my throat and pray to God I'm doing the right thing.

"Enzo, it's Malcolm."

"Mal, good to hear from ya. Everything okay at the hospital? You and the zoo of animals good?"

I fight to control the emotions because Frankie's family was supposed to be mine too, but again it took just one day to fuck everything up.

"Yeah, Enzo, work is good. That's why I'm calling. I need to tell you something and ask you a question. First, a patient was brought in from the prison earlier today due to an episode inside, and two prisoners were severely injured. I hate to say it but, Enzo, one of the prisoners was one of the men from back then. I didn't want him to see me but because he's an asshole and started trouble, I went in and stopped him, along with help from my boss. My worry is if the other is not in jail or dead, don't want him to find Frankie. No, I'm not asking for her number, just want to make sure she's safe. Can you reach out and make sure?"

"Damn, Mal. Yeah, I'll have Billie reach out once we're done. Now what's the question, son?"

Knowing I'm opening myself up to a world of pain, it needs to be done. I can't keep living in the past. As much as it hurts, this is another process of healing, or that's what my therapist has told me time and time again. Why I think this is the right time, who knows? Here goes nothing.

"Enzo, I need you to be honest. Is she happy? I mean truly engaged and enjoying her life? If you tell me yes then I'll try to move on, but something deep in my gut is telling me she's not. You know we had that once in a lifetime connection and that's what I'm going off of. No one can compare to Frankie, but I will try to move forward 'cause I want her happy."

The other end of the phone line is quiet, then I hear boots hitting the floor as Enzo moves away from his grandchildren. A door squeaks open then slams shut.

"Mal, if you ever tell my Billie I told you this, I swear to God and all of my Italian ancestors that I will make sure you suffer before going in your grave deep in the ocean's floor. Personally, I don't think our Frankie has been happy since right before those degenerates ruined both of your lives. Billie and I were just talking about maybe getting Frankie to tell us where she is so we can visit her. Problem is, she's so afraid of being found by the wrong people. Shit, Mal, hang on, got another call. Well, what the shit… it's Frankie. Give me a minute, son."

I start to pace waiting for Enzo to return to our call. Minute by minute goes by as I listen to nothing. My dogs, Buddy and Chloe, start to pace with me while the cats ignore the shit outta me and bathe themselves. Must be five minutes before I hear the line engage.

"Mal, you still there?"

"Yeah, Enzo. Goddamn, it's driving me crazy. She okay? Did you find out where she's living? Come on, please just spit it out, man."

I hear him walking around, calling for his wife, Billie. These two, damn, what they've been through and are still strong and together. Enzo is an Italian whose parents brought him to the States when he was a young boy. Billie is an African American woman who grew up in New York. Frankie and her siblings got the best of both. When I hear Enzo tell Billie it's me on the phone and I hear her yell, "Hey, Malcolm." She's one of the few besides her daughter, who when not calling me by the nickname she gave me, uses my full name. Enzo is whispering but when Billie lets out a loud gasp, I'm about ready to jump in my vehicle and drive to their house.

"Mal, hey, sorry, wanted to fill Billie in. Now, do you work tomorrow? Or better question, you got any vacation time, son? The reason for Frankie's call is someone is out there looking and asking about her. Someone she knows took a picture of the guy and yeah, son, Frankie says it's one of the men from... you know. I begged, pleaded, and threatened until she told me where she was and what she's been up to. Get this, son, she's part of an all-female motorcycle club in somewhere called Timber-Ghost, Montana. Billie is right now on her computer trying to book us flights. You in? And no, I didn't tell her I had you on hold or you called worried about her. Personally, it's time you two get your heads outta your asses and talk. No, don't give me none of your bullshit, son. So, are you in or out?"

My mind is going in twenty directions. Yeah, I have quite a bit of vacation time, though I also have five fur babies. Can't just up and leave. Before I can say a word, Enzo cuts into my thoughts.

"Mal, Billie has Shamonda on the phone. Our youngest daughter can't go because of being seven and a half months pregnant. She just told her mother she can come and stay at your place and take care of your house full of animals. She'll bring her two older kids since her husband has been deployed. Because she's pregnant, she can have her boys clean the litter pails. You still got the three cats, right? So if that was what was holding you back, am I telling my wife to get a ticket for you too? No, don't go there, Mal, we got it. Make a list of what needs to be done to take care of the cats. You still got Buddy and Chloe, right? Damn, we haven't seen them in a while, they gotta be getting' up in age. Shit, as usual, my mind goes in all directions. Hang on. What, Billie? Yeah, get Mal a ticket. What time? Woman, are you fuc... I mean, frigging nuts? Oh, okay, that works better. Mal, be here tomorrow by four forty-five in the morning. Plane takes off at eight fifty-five. Since Tharon is back home yet again, that little bastard can drive us to the airport. Any questions?"

I shake my head then, realizing Enzo can't see me do that so I tell him no. He tells me to try and relax, we'll get some answers tomorrow. Once we say our goodbyes, I go to the office and start up my computer. Then I start my list of how to take care of my fur babies. No one has ever had to watch them—well, yeah, they did—when I had my third surgery. My sister was living with me at the time so the dogs and cats were used to her. Hopefully, Shamonda will be able to handle the crazy I call home.

After making and printing my lists with where everything is and what to do, I head to my master bedroom to pack while I try to envision how this is going to go. No matter what runs through my head, one thing I know for certain. This time I'm not letting Frankie go without a fight.

FOUR
'WILDCAT'
FRANKIE

Lying in my bed, I'm afraid to get out of it. Yesterday's shitshow left me feeling raw and way too vulnerable, which are two emotions I try hard to avoid. Then to top it off, after just about every Devil's Handmaidens sister managed to spoon or cuddle with me, except the two ready to burst, the questions started getting deep and I was truly starting to panic; Taz faked going into labor. I was shocked because she actually seemed to be experiencing the beginning stages of labor. Then one of the prospects called Enforcer—and shit—our calm, crystal-loving sister became like her namesake: Tasmanian Devil. That colored hair of hers was flying all over. Poor Kitty didn't know what she did wrong until Taz got in her face and instead of explaining she immediately broke out sobbing.

The only good thing is it took the spotlight off me. When Enforcer and Teddy burst through the door, one look and the man looked at the boy-child and said…

"Teddy, Momma's playing around again. Come on, let's get back to the dogs." Then they both turned around and left as fast as they got there. Everyone watched Taz, who was staring right at me. When I studied her face, she kinda giggled then winked at me. Motherfucker, she was faking to get them off my back. I rushed toward Taz, grabbing and pulling her into me as much as I could with her pregnant belly in the way. It was one of the nicest things anyone has ever done for me and I whispered it in her ear. She leaned over and whispered back to me.

"You haven't seen anything yet, Wildcat. Prepare— the wild winds are shifting, be strong, and lean on those around you, stay focused on the prize at the end, and never give up on your dreams."

The way she said it had the hair on the back of my neck standing up. I know Taz truly believes in her crystals, cards, incense, sage and everything else that is natural and earthy, but it isn't something I've ever gotten into. When she grabbed my hand and placed something heavy in it, I look down then I close my fingers and felt two stones.

"Black tourmaline is for protection, inner power, and confidence. Clear quartz for grounding, inner energy, and concentration. Always keep these on you. I've cleansed them but you can put them in that selenite bowl I gave you to be sure no negative energy from me passes down to you. I love you, Wildcat. We all do. Now, I got to go make peace with my man and man-child. Why did I pick such an astute male to be in my life when

I already had Teddy? Though not complaining too much. Call me if you need anything."

She raised her hand and caressed my cheek then turned and walked out while our other sisters watched her. I remember vividly that Taz is not one for drama or large displays of anything. She is usually balanced and calm, so guess it's true what they say about the hormones of pregnancy.

One by one my club sisters make their way to leaving, giving me a hug, squeeze, or knuckle bump, trying to let me know I'm not alone. That's the thing about the Devil's Handmaidens club, it's about sisterhood, first and foremost, with our club sisters but then it extends to any woman who needs guidance or assistance. When it's only Tink, Glory, and Shadow, I gulp. Guess it's time to explain in-depth what freaked me out. Glory walks to the door, closing and locking it. Damn, our VP does pay attention, just hearing the locks makes me feel better, even with these women in the room. Doubt anyone would get past Shadow, but the deadliest one is probably Glory with Tink not far behind.

We all take a seat either on the huge extra-long couch or in a wingback chair. My hands are twisting together, well, that's until Tink grabs them, holding on tightly.

"Sister, there isn't anything that can destroy you unless you let it into your head to fester. Now, take some breaths. Zoey, get her some water. When you're ready, Wildcat, tell us what freaked you out and what might be heading our way. Hey, no judgment, sister. We can deal with anything if we know what it is. I know some of it, but let's start at the beginning."

So after a couple of minutes that's exactly what I do. I try my damnedest to leave nothing out, no matter how painful or soul wrecking it is. I must give Tink, Glory, and Shadow kudos because no one, not even our enforcer, interrupts me at any time. They just sit close to me, always making sure one or the other has a hand on mine or bumping my shoulder or when Shadow sits on the floor, pulla my legs around her, and hugs me at a particular hard moment in my story. I feel Tink's eyes on me every time I speak Malcolm's name. It is kind of eerie because those green eyes seem to be looking into my soul.

Not sure for how long I talk, but when I finish a steaming cup of tea is placed in front of me. When I look up, Glory gives me a soft smile. I know the stories of these women but to have both Tink and Glory running this club, there are no two women who fit together better. Shadow kneels in front of me, squeezing my knees before standing up. Tink is on the move too, walking to the small kitchen, opening the fridge, and grabbing some waters. Then she heads directly to the table.

Everyone follows our prez's lead and heads over to the small dinette. The silence is relaxing and for some reason I feel lighter. Maybe from getting all that shit out by telling my story, knowing whatever Tink has to say it's not just for the good of our club. The Devil's Handmaidens is a one-percent motorcycle club. But our mission is to rescue those being victimized or abused. Funny how each and every one of us in the club has a past that includes being a victim of some kind of abuse. Who better to understand the effects than a prior victim? Though we are also survivors since we as a group can work together to help other victims become survivors.

"Wildcat, we all know how hard that was. Thank you for sharing with us. Not sure why we continue to attract trouble when all we ever want to do is live a good life while helping others. Saying that, this is what I think our next steps should be. First, we get Raven to start going over some of the cameras in town. I know you don't have names and stuff like that, so maybe our technology specialist will be able to give us an idea about who we are dealing with. This is the hard part, Wildcat, for you. I think it's in everyone's best interest if you reach out to your family. Give them a warning. Also maybe give Malcolm a heads-up. Now, hold on, sister. Before you lose your shit, think about it if the roles were reversed. Would Malcolm leave you hanging when trouble was knocking at his door? From what you've told us about him, I'm going to guess he's one of the 'nice guys.' Try to look past whatever is holding you back from him. He is not the enemy sister. That's all I'm saying."

I know she's right, that's what's pissing me off though. Not saying it's going to happen, but with me telling my story and putting the truth out there, just maybe I'll be able to move forward. Though my club helps victims out, I want to do even more. It's a secret dream of mine but, and I hate to even think it, just maybe something will come of my application and I can become a deputy for Timber-Ghost. That is, if Sheriff George thinks I'm the right candidate for the job.

"Now that's the Wildcat we love to see. That grin on your face with the fire in your eyes. Whatcha thinking about there, sister?"

My head jerks as I realize I went off into a daydream with my eyes wide open. I lean back, shifting my eyes to Shadow, who's smirking my way. Yeah, our enforcer has come a long way, but sometimes she's still like a kid trying to mess with others. I know she's trying to take my mind off all this unexpected bullshit that's landed in my lap, and for that I so love her.

"Shadow, feel the same about you every time I see you and Panther together or notice that special dreamy look you get in your eyes when you think about him. But more than that, I see how far you've come and that's what I want in my life, though that can't happen until all this bullshit is over and done. You hear me?"

* * *

Well, it wasn't bad enough I had to relive that time with my club sisters, but then I reached out to my family to have them freaking the ever-loving hell out. I could hear it in my parents' voices, though they tried to hide it. So I finally broke down, after all this time, to tell them where I was and what I was doing with my life. They told me somehow, someway, they would be out here so we can figure this out together. Guess Malcolm had told my parents one of the assholes from that day ended up in the emergency room from taking a beating in the prison where he was serving time. That news didn't bother me as much as me not knowing my parents still had some kind of relationship and contact with Malcolm. I'm not mad though, I'm more sad than anything. This whole situation is messed up and seems to be on a downward spiral. Only time will tell. Told my parents to let Malcolm know whenever they either see or speak to him what was going on in Montana, though I asked—no, begged—them not to give him any specifics. Can't undo that broken road, that's for sure. *He made his choice*.

That's the last thought I have before I fall into a restless sleep, not knowing tomorrow will be bringing my past to meet my present. And what a meeting it will turn out to be.

FIVE
'MALCOLM'
MALTY

I'm about ready to lose my mind. Why is this flight taking so long? We need to get to Bumfuck, Montana, not five plus hours later. We started this trip at the crack of dawn and have just kept running into issues and delays. Finally, we're about to land in Billings, Montana, though I've been told it's a couple of hours' drive to Timber-Ghost, which is where Frankie has put down roots.

Just thinking about her name gives me goosebumps. It always makes me angry because of how we parted ways. I know most of it falls on my shoulders, for sure. I wasn't in a good place so instead of being honest and trying to explain it to Frankie, I blew my stack time and time again. I took it out on her, especially seeing how badly injured she was, which had a part of me die because I didn't protect her from the deranged assholes who found us in the woods that day. The worst part though is she knows everything that happened to me, and that right there killed me. I've not shared with many people what happened on that day. Well, doctors and my immediate family know. Oh, and Frankie's family knows because after I chased her off, they stood by me. Especially her parents. There was a brief moment when the prognosis wasn't good, and I seriously thought I was going to die. That's when I realized what I'd done to Frankie was so wrong.

So here I am now, trying to make amends while trying to do what I didn't do back then, protect her. After her parents spoke to her, we all decided to make this trip. Thank God for Shamonda, who, with her two boys, is now staying at my place to watch over all my fur babies. It gave me so much relief when she came over late last night with four suitcases, telling me she wanted to spend the night with me. Then she burst out in laughter when I heard her older boy groan loudly.

"Malcolm, you should have seen your face. Please tell me you've gotten some since you pushed Frankie away? Because if you haven't, that's a waste of good one-hundred-percent prime male, if you know what I mean."

That had me busting a gut. Shamonda hasn't changed at all, though she seems to be hiding something. Obviously, it isn't that she is way pregnant, I could see that with my own eyes. She wanted to know all about me but when I asked back about her life, she changed the subject. Her two boys took to all the animals. Her older one, Jackson, loved the cats while Jr. fell for both Buddy and Chloe, my two rescues. Then we got down to introducing her to my crazy bunch of fur babies. By the time she was set up in one of my spare rooms and the boys in another, it was early morning. I didn't sleep hardly at all. When I stepped into the kitchen, talk about being shocked to see not only Shamonda in there, but also Vernell and Tharon. Vernell is Frankie's older sister and Tharon is the baby of the family.

It was like old home week. Shamonda had coffee already made and Vernell took to making breakfast. I caught up with Frankie's siblings and could tell how much they missed her. Tharon took me off to the side and told me I had to fix this shit so Frankie could come back home. When the doorbell rang at four fifteen, I quickly made my way to the door. Looking out the side glass, I can't believe my eyes. No way in hell. Swinging the door open, a bull of a man grabs me and gives me a bear hug. All I get to do is grunt.

"Motherfucker, what... your phone broke? Haven't talked to you in what two, no, three months. Then last night you send that crazy as fuck text so I cleared my schedule. I'm going with ya. No, don't give me your lip, said I'm going. You ready? If I remember anything correctly from back in the day, I'm sure Billie told you that if you were late, she was leaving without you, though now it's a us."

I stand here staring at one of my best friends.

Michael and I go way back. He was there when I needed a friend. Or when I thought I couldn't go on. So to see him standing at the door to pick me up while Frankie's family is behind me, I feel the emotions rising. Fuck, don't want to lose it in front of everyone. Leave it to Michael to see through my bullshit.

"All right, give the man some space. Go on, we'll be back to say our goodbyes. No, Shamonda, don't want to hear your sass. We got to go woman, so give us a minute."

Reluctantly, they all turn and head back to the kitchen. When we are alone, Michael is staring at me intently. I wait for it and he doesn't make me wait too long.

"How you holding up, brother? No, don't try to make it less than what this is. Been telling you for a long goddamn time to fix it, but did you listen... hell to the no. Well, the good man upstairs is now going to make you do what you should have years ago. So take your minute. I'm going to go bust Sharonda's chops because I can. Then we've got to go. You of all people know Frankie's mom means it when she's says she'll leave your ass behind."

He walks past me, giving me a small push so he can shut the door. Then like he's done it before; he swaggers his way to my kitchen, which is where he'll stir the pot—nope, in his case the shit—for sure. Not sure what is up with him and Shamonda, not my business. Though I do know he'd never disrespect her husband, Dewayne, in any way. I take a few deep breaths, feeling a bit better that Michael will be with me every step of the way. Couldn't ask for a better friend. I go back upstairs to grab my carry-on and small suitcase. I place them by the front door then go toward the kitchen, where I can hear all kinds of laughter. It hits me at that moment how quiet and depressing this house has been. Just hearing the chaos in my kitchen makes me swear, no matter what happens in Montana, I'm going to start living again… not just existing.

*** * ***

What a fucking clusterfuck. Jesus Christ, if it could go wrong, it did. First off, neither of Frankie's parents told her we were coming out to Buttfuck, Montana. They wanted to surprise her and got pissed at me when I strongly disagreed. Billie told me then it was her way or the highway, since I didn't have a clue where Frankie was living. Then she got pissed at Michael for who knows what and told him he wasn't coming. She told him after she tried to get him a ticket the flight was booked, so he would have to stay home. He calmly told her he booked his flight last night after my text. Then she got pissed because Tharon was with Shamonda and not ready to drive us to the airport. Michael again told her he took care of it as a stretch limousine pulled up in front of the house. That brought a small smile to Billie's face. Then when we go to the airport, somehow, they messed up the reservations and instead of a direct flight we had a layover. So needless to say, at this moment, all of our nerves are beyond frayed. Thank the gods for Michael. He's been the glue holding us all together with his calm demeanor and crazy as fuck jokes that had both Billie and Enzo laughing instead of screaming or crying.

When our connecting flight was ready to board, I once again tried to talk to Billie to maybe let Frankie know. She broke down and told me she put a call into the Devil's Handmaidens Motorcycle Club and spoke to a very nice young lady named Hannah, who told her someone would pick us up at the airport and drive all of us into Timber-Ghost. That put me at ease a little bit, but still I had a nagging feeling no one was sharing what was going on with Frankie. And if she is still even half of what she was when we were together, she was not fond of surprises at all. As we take our seats, I see Michael using his charm with two of the flight attendants. When Billie walks by she mutters something to the effect of, "Why did you bring that dog with? You know he's going to try and get those girls into the bathroom for a mile-high hookup." I glance at her and she's smirking my way, so guess she's not truly seriously mad or upset. I mean, she's known him as long as she's known me, for Christ's sake. Enzo walks by me giving me a fist bump and mouthing, "Thanks."

As the flight comes to an end and we are told to fasten our seat belts as we descend into Billings, Montana, I can feel the tingling on the back of my neck. From sitting so long the muscles along my spine are screaming, but I wasn't going to miss this trip for anything. I have my collapsible walking cane if I need it, but would prefer Frankie to see me after all this time as a whole man, not like the asshole I was when I sent her away. That day has haunted me for the last couple of years. I wasn't in my right mind and she knew exactly what happened to me, if I'm honest with myself, I was so embarrassed and ashamed. And since I've never really taken the time necessary to deal with those feelings, I'm carrying that bullshit along with me, though I continue to fight to stay in control. From behind me I hear a "Mal" so I turn to see both Billie and Enzo looking my way. It's Billie who called my name, so I wait to see what she wants.

"Son, now remember, no matter what our Frankie says, know one thing…she still loves you, though you broke her when you told her to go away. No, I don't say that to hurt you, Malcolm, just to prepare you for the fight ahead. We both support you and will do whatever it takes, but don't let her words discourage you. That's one of the reasons we didn't tell our daughter we were coming out here. She would have found any of a thousand excuses on why we shouldn't then if she knew for certain we were coming, she would have taken off. Trust the 'mature' folks, Malcolm, we have our reasons for what we do. Now when we land, we are to go to the main area and Hannah said she'd be waiting for us. Keep your eyes open. Oh, and tell Michael to wipe that grin off his face. I saw him strut out of the bathroom after that little redheaded flight attendant. Dog, that is what he is."

Enzo tries to hide his laughter but can't until Billie

gives him the stink eye. Then he turns his head to look out the window, still trying to hide his grin. As we descend, even though I don't do it often anymore, I say a little prayer that everything goes well and we don't make it worse for Frankie because from what I've heard, she's kind of rebuilt her life. Which hurts, though it's my fault. I sent her away but didn't think she'd ever, for one, go, and two, build a life without me. Yeah, I've had some, I don't know what you call them, hookups… but nothing serious. I don't even know if she's married, has a partner or kids. That would totally suck but this is the next step in my healing, I guess. One day—nope, one hour—at a time. As Judy, my boss, told me when I called for some vacation time.

"Malcolm, it's about damn time. Take as much as you need and come back to me whole. That's all I ask. No, you've never done anything wrong at work but you are going through life barely living, my friend. Find yourself again, Mal. You've got so much potential. Keep in touch and let me know when you think you'll be back. For now, I have you out for four weeks, which doesn't even touch all of the available time off you have banked."

So here I am trying to "find myself" and take back what was taken from me. Not sure how that's going to go, but shit, what do I have to lose? I feel his eyes before I even look to the left. Michael is watching me like a hawk.

"You got this, Mal. And I'm here to have your back. No regrets, remember?"

Shit, that was what we always said to each other

growing up. No matter what happened. So looking at him, I nod and give it right back.

"Damn straight, Michael. No fucking regrets."

That brings a smile to his face and a slap to the back of my head from Billie behind me. *Damn, nothing ever changes*, I think to myself as I grin back at my best friend.

SIX
'SQUIRT'
HANNAH

When I got that call from Wildcat's mom, I immediately reached out to Tink and Glory. After explaining what I was told, my prez said I was to take Dani and Dottie with me to the airport to pick them up. Now since we have our van and one of the SUVs, I decided on taking the extra-long passenger van, which will give us some room. Dani is following with the smaller SUV for some of the folks coming out this way. Since Dani and Dottie are attached at the hip being twins, I reached out to Presley to see if he wanted to come with. So we have three Devil's Handmaidens and one Intruder, all of us prospects. Yeah, we draw attention, but hey, that's who we are.

Presley's been quiet, not sure what's up his ass, but as my auntie Zoey taught me, don't beg for a man's attention. So as hard as it is I just continue to drive, listening to the radio. When we are just about at the entrance for pickup, he turns the radio down. I glance his way and see how serious he looks. Oh shit, is he going to break up with me while I'm driving? That I won't be able to handle. I'm still really worried about Wildcat and what's going on, don't need boyfriend issues too.

"Hannah, babe, what's going on between us? I mean, we barely see each other and you seem like I'm bothering you when we are together. Is there someone else you got those gorgeous green eyes on? Just be honest, it'll tear the fuck out of me but I gotta know."

Thank God I catch a light coming off the highway. I turn to him, slight surprise I'm sure all over my face.

"Presley, my God, our club has been through the wringer the last year and a half or so. We are barely catching our breaths and now some shit from Wildcat's past somehow found her here. No, I don't have my eyes on anyone else, you goof. You are it for me, but if you are looking around at some of the easy girls who are in Timber-Ghost, or those sweet butts at your club, don't let me hold you back. You knew I wasn't easy, Presley, when we met and nothing has changed."

I can feel his anger but at that moment the light changes so I start to go through the intersection. He doesn't say another word and neither do I. Something is eating at him and I'm not sure what. Maybe he should just be honest and tell me what's on his mind. That's when I get an idea.

"Hey, don't be mad at me. Yeah, we've been distracted lately and that's to be expected the longer we are together, and with all we have to do within our clubs. I know my dad, Tank, is riding your ass and I'm sorry for that. He's just worried that you might hurt me. Damn it, Presley, you know what's been going on, I don't have to tell you. Dad and Mom have been through the wringer, not to mention both have been injured. It's taken them longer to heal, then Dad goes and has a heart attack. Life is starting to get back to normal. Let's get through this Wildcat drama and then we can talk. 'Kay? You know I care about you, don't you?"

He reaches over and grabs my hand. I squeeze his and that's how we drive to the pickup area of the airport, holding hands. Now usually, the airports don't want you to leave your vehicle and go into the terminal but because of who we are and what we do, most of the security guards know us. So I park and get out, leaving Presley standing by the van. Dottie also gets out, leaving Dani standing by the SUV. I forgot the sign so I rush back to the van, opening the side door and grabbing it. Before I can go, Presley pulls me close and kisses the snot out of me. Before I can pull him close, he lets me go with a kiss on the nose. When I turn to leave, he cracks my ass hard, but the burn isn't all bad as I begin to tingle in all the really good places. Damn, does that man get to me. It's been so rough not giving in, though he's not pressuring me—never has. I just want to make sure when I do give my V away, it's the right guy at the right time since once it's gone, that's it. I want it to mean something, not just be sex and getting off.

Dottie and I enter the airport and stand off to the

side. I have the sign at my side, waiting for the passengers to start coming down the escalator. Dottie asks me what I think about what's going on, and we start to talk about the situation with Wildcat. I keep glancing back and forth toward the escalator because I don't want to miss our sister's family. When I hear Dottie let out a small "Holy shit," I turn my head and almost drop the sign as I see an older version of Wildcat with a very handsome older man. Behind them are two gorgeous guys. Both are hot, though one knows it and it shows, while the other is more reserved. I raise the sign just as the reserved one starts looking around. He points to us and the older couple, once off the moving stairs, makes their way to us. I lean the sign against the wall. The older woman approaches me, hand out.

"Hannah? Hi, I'm Billie, this is Enzo. We're Frankie's parents. This is Malcolm. Not sure you know who he is, but he and Frankie go way back. And that rogue is Michael."

I hear Dottie snicker at what Billie said. Michael immediately moves his eyes from me to check out Dottie. And check out he does, from head to toe and back up. Dottie gives it right back until I shoulder bump her. Then I give my attention to Wildcat's parents.

"It's a pleasure to meet you both. Yes, I'm Hannah, but my club's name is Squirt. This is another prospect, Dottie. We have our vehicles outside, ready to take you to the ranch."

The woman looks to her husband and the younger man named Malcolm. He steps forward and I can tell he's either uncomfortable or in pain, though not sure why.

"Hi, Hannah, I mean, Squirt, call me Mal. We were going to check into a hotel and maybe grab something to eat before we spring this surprise on Frankie. Any suggestions?"

"Mal, our prez would skin us alive if we didn't take you back to the ranch. There are en suites in the main house and a few empty cabins behind, so you can have your pick. We figured once y'all are settled, we can pop back into town as Wildcat is managing our club bar and grill—The Wooden Spirits. Can probably grab a bite to eat there. Nice to meet you, sorry it's under these circumstances. I was the one who brought this to Wildcat, as I was at the coffee shop when the guy was asking questions about her. Something about him didn't sit right with me, so I took a picture and went right to her. The rest is history."

The other guy, Michael, comes forward, his hand stretched out toward me. I take it and he shakes, giving me a million-dollar smile. Then he turns to Dottie, doing the same thing. Something about Michael is off, like he's trying too hard to impress. As we all get acquainted, my gut tells me whatever went down involved Wildcat, Malcolm, and maybe even Michael, I'm not sure. I know Wildcat was explaining in great detail the situation to Tink, Glory, and Shadow. I'm sure we'll all be filled in when the time is right. My job is to get these folks back to the ranch, so that's what I'm going to do.

"Does anyone have checked luggage? If not, let's get

moving so we don't hit a ton of traffic. Have any of you been to Big Sky Country before? Sorry, that's what we call the state of Montana. So if no one has been out here, you're in for a treat. Best place in the world to live, though that's my opinion. Wait 'til you see the mountains and wildflowers growing all over. Let's get the luggage in the SUV with Dottie and Dani. Miss Billie, Mr. Enzo, you can take the bucket seats in the van, they are comfortable. Mal and Michael can sit in the third row, should be enough leg room."

Michael is the last to come toward the vans. He looks to the one I'm driving with Presley leaning—well-now he's standing—arms crossed on his kutte, looking either pissed or jealous. Not sure, thought we settled his nerves about us. Michael must read his expression because he grins before coming to me, leaning down to whisper in my ear.

"Do you mind, Hannah, if I ride with the twins? Gives you time to get to know Frankie's family a bit. And it will give me a quick minute to get to know Dottie, I mean Dottie and Dani."

I laugh because, man, does he have game. And he smells so good, though not as good as Presley does. I nod and tell him to go ahead if my sisters don't have a problem with him riding along. He goes to talk to the twins as I watch Presley help Billie into the van, then he shuts the door after the men are in. He turns to me, so I walk up to him.

"Want me to drive, Hannah, so you can talk to them? I don't mind at all, really."

I put my hands on his waist and lift on my toes to gently kiss his lips. I can tell he's kind of shocked because I'm not too big on public displays of affection, or PDA, as us young people call it. I'm doing this to claim him in front of the other guys and to put him at ease. When his hands pull me closer, I let him. Just as we start to kiss deeper, I hear a shout from Dottie.

"Would you two get a room already? Fu.... I mean, damn, let's get moving, Squirt."

Pulling apart, I smile at her while giving her the finger, which she promptly returns. I look up at Presley and wink, which has him laughing. Then he walks me to the passenger door, opens it for me, and helps me in. After slamming it shut, he walks around the front of the van and gets into the driver's seat.

"So are we ready to get this party on the road, people? Next stop is the ranch but if ya have any questions, please don't hesitate to ask. This is going to take about two plus hours or so, depending on traffic. Relax and in that cooler between the seats there are waters, pops, and teas, if anyone wants one. Also, we have some granola bars and fruit in the burlap shopping bag. Help yourselves."

As Presley pulls out, I look back to see Wildcat's mom and dad looking around, but it's Malcolm who catches my eye. He seems extremely nervous so I give him a tiny grin, which he nods at. Well, guess we'll just have to wait and see how this plays out. One thing I know for certain is, our prez didn't tell Wildcat she's about to have guests. Not sure I'd have played it like that, but that's why Tink's the prez. Fingers crossed she's doing the right thing. *We will see,* I think to myself as Billie hands me two waters, one for Presley and one for me.

SEVEN
'WILDCAT'
FRANKIE

Shit, I'm running on damn fumes at the moment. For some reason we are once again swamped at the Wooden Spirits tonight, and it's not even the weekend yet. No live music or anything, but just about every table is full of folks and the bar area is hopping. And for some reason there is an unusual number of Devil's Handmaidens here. I mean, yeah, we all come to eat here at times as we have the best cook, who can put together a badass plate of food. Though tonight something is up. I can feel it in my gut, just don't know what. Shadow, Glory, and Taz are in my office in the back. Taz has her feet up because the edema in her feet seems to be getting worse day by day.

Peanut is busting her ass yet again. We need to talk; she needs to get someone else for her team to help if we continue to be so busy. Well, some of the sisters help when necessary but we need a permanent person to help her. Kiwi's at the bar while Heartbreaker is jumping to keep up with the tables. I see Kitty giving Peanut a hand, which is great.

When I turn around, I see Vixen at a table taking an order. Well, holy fuck, when did our road captain start waiting tables? I watch as she leans from foot to foot. I'm guessing her huge pregnant belly is starting to bother her. Not sure what's got her up and about, but she's about to pop. And so is Taz, that's why I know something ain't right for both to be here. With that thought, I turn to see Teddy and Olivia, as usual holding hands, coming toward me. When they reach me, Olivia steps forward and gives me a hug while Teddy's eyes take me in. Damn, every time he's around, I get this feeling of security and peace. Weird coming from a kid, but hey, weirder shit has happened.

"Auntie Wildcat, have you seen my momma? Dad is outside talking to Yoggie and Noodles but we're starving, so maybe we can get Momma to talk to the cook to feed us. I mean, we'll even clean our messy dishes up, promise."

Teddy is so frigging adorable. I lean down to their level first. Then give it to them both.

"Follow me, let's get you both into the kitchen and at the special table in there. I believe, if you ask nicely, the cook will make her all-time, awesome grilled cheese sandwiches for you."

They both grin and nod their little heads. I make my way past everyone and head toward the kitchen when a little hand grabs mine. Thinking it's Olivia, I look down to see it's Teddy. Something tells me to lean down toward him, so I do.

"Auntie Wildcat, I'm always around if you need anything. I might not be like all the other kids, but I do love you very much. Momma tells me to always be honest and that's what I'm doing. Hang on, I brought this for you."

I watch as he reaches in his pocket, pulling out one of the pretty little bags Taz always has on her. Inside I can see maybe a disc or circle. Teddy reaches inside and pulls out a black cord with something hanging from it. When he hands it to me, I can then make out it's some form of a necklace with a shit, what does Taz call it? I take a second or two when it comes to me—a tree of life in a circle made of crystals. Then Teddy continues.

"Momma says the tree of life helps with the connection between past and present. Wear it all the time, Auntie Wildcat. I hope you like it as Momma and I made it."

For some reason I get very emotional but under Teddy and Olivia's watchful eyes, I put the necklace on. When he smiles, I reach down and very carefully give him a kiss on the top of his head. Being that Teddy is autistic, we are all very careful in our approach to him. With therapy and the interaction of the club, he's come a long way. Once I'm done kissing on him, we make our way back to the kitchen, where our cook gets busy making two special plates for these two very special kids.

* * *

Damn, I don't think this night is ever going to end. I mean, it's not even nine o'clock but with the way my body feels, you'd think I've been working for twenty-four hours straight. Kiwi is in the kitchen helping our cook catch up on orders, while Heartbreaker is manning the bar and waitressing. Peanut is busy cleaning up. Now to my utter surprise while Taz and Vixen are sitting down sipping on lemon water, Shadow is helping at the bar—save us all—and Glory is backup in the kitchen. My God, am I in an alternate universe? Why is just about every Devil's Handmaidens sister at the Wooden Spirits tonight? And the looks I'm getting are starting to freak me out. Just when I'm about to ask one of them what's up, Tink comes toward me with a serious as fuck face on. In one of our large circular booths off to the left I see Noodles, Panther, Yoggie, Enforcer, and Avalanche. Oh wait, here comes Ironside pulling a chair to the edge of the booth. *The gang's all here* runs through my head while I wait for whatever Tink's about to say.

That's when I feel them all getting close. First the waddlers approach. Somehow both Vixen and Taz manage to grab a small table close to where we are. Then Shadow and Glory, along with—well, shit—when did Raven and Duchess get here? Finally, Rebel, Kiwi, and Heartbreaker step out of the kitchen and start to come our way. Tink waits for them all to surround me. Just when she's about to talk, Peanut and Kitty come our way almost running, waving their hands.

"Tink, Squirt is about to pull up. Just wanted you to know."

The feeling in my gut is spreading. Haven't had this feeling since when I was a recruit cop back home. The hair on the back of my neck is standing up, I'm sure. Before I can ask what the fuck is going on, Tink turns back first, looking around at each sister then at me. That's when it hits me that somehow the bar and grill is filled with just us and our family. The patrons who were in here maybe ten or fifteen minutes ago are gone. I start to move backward but Shadow is right there. When I go to move around Tink, Glory is there to stop me. Then before I can think about what I'm about to say, I lose it.

"What the hell is going on? Why are you all closing in on me? You're making me nervous, like something bad is about to happen. Did you find something out about that guy Squirt saw? Did you track him down, Raven? Come on, talk to me, please. This is making me utterly crazy, as you can tell, because I never lose control. Can someone tell me why this is happening?"

Tink moves closer and grabs my hands. Now our prez is extremely petite, but the strength just in the way she's holding my hands gives me a moment of peace in my scattered thoughts. Until she opens her mouth.

"Wildcat, what I'm about to say is probably going to piss you the fuck off. Not our intention but after we spoke with you, decided that you needed this. If we're wrong, I'll apologize now and later, but in about I don't know, four or five minutes, there are some folks who are going to walk in here to see you. How you react is on you, but know they've come a long way to make sure you're okay. No, give me a few more seconds. Raven has been working and has gotten closer, but apparently this asshole has found somewhere to hide out that isn't on the radar. Both Raven and Freak have been working on this since Squirt told us yesterday. They will give us an update tomorrow afternoon at the ranch, in our meeting room. Until then you're off the clock. Nope, don't argue with me on this, Wildcat. We love you, sister, always have. Oh shit, okay. Well, it's time. Remember what our club is about and maybe you'll understand why we did what we did."

I look at her and turn to look at my other club sisters when the door opens and I see Squirt, Dottie, Dani, and oh my God... my mom and dad. Before I can think, I'm pushing my way to them as they are moving quickly my way. When I feel my dad's arms around me, I start to cry silently. Until Mom pushes in between us, tears running down her face.

"What the heck? How did you find me and so quickly? We just talked yesterday. Mom, don't cry. I'm okay, see... everything is okay."

Something, not sure what, has me look up and past my mom, and that's when I see him. My God, I can't believe he's here. He's more handsome than I remember, and damn, he's grown into that body of his. I'm afraid to look into his beautiful multifaceted green-blue-grayish eyes, in case they have that look from when he told me *to get the fuck outta his hospital room and keep walking out the door and his life. And take these problems with me.* When I get the courage up to look at him, I see he's not only staring at me but his eyes are glistening. What the hell? And behind him is his bestie, Michael. He's also watching me but with a different look. A wary kind of on-guard stare, which I don't fully get. He was never a one-hundred-percent fan of mine. Probably the cop issue, though as far as I know he's never been in trouble with the law but some of his friends have, big time. When I see Squirt making her way to me, I move away from my mom and dad. She comes right to me and squeezes me tightly in her little arms.

"If you want, I'll make them leave. Tink told us not to tell you and we all knew why. If you had a clue your folks and Malcolm were on their way here, you'd have run away and never would have come back to us. This way you have all of us for support and your family, so together we can figure out what to do next. And damn, Wildcat, he's hot. That's him, right?"

That brings a small smile to my face. Leave it to Hannah to break through the dark mood. She has such a way about her. A little of Tink, a bit of Tank, and mainly Momma Diane. I love this little sister so much and she's been through the wringer and came out the other side still smiling, with those twinkling green eyes that seem to miss nothing. She has the same spidey senses as Shadow, which is scary as they aren't even related. Though our enforcer found her in a hole in the ground being held there by her biological father. No one ever found out what he planned to do with her. He kidnapped her when she was a child and Shadow found her when she was nearly nineteen. Only God knows what she saw in all that time. But she still is so innocent in many ways, thank Christ.

With my eyes on Hannah—nope, gotta get used to calling her Squirt—I didn't see my Mal… No, what the hell? I mean, Malcolm move closer. When I hear a deep raspy throat clear, I can feel him before a word comes out of his mouth. I feel my body reacting to him being close and part of me is glad to see I'm still alive, because the very few times I've tried to be with a man there was nothing. It was like that part of me was dead. Well, it just woke the fuck up for sure, if the way my body is reacting is a sign. My nipples are hard peaks and between my legs is getting wetter by the minute. Shit, can you believe I'm turned on during one of the most intense moments in my entire life? Should have known all I needed was my Malcolm.

Then I hear that voice and I can swear half of my club sisters sigh at his tone, which I like because of the natural gravelly growl in it. I don't want to but I look up into those stunning colorful eyes of his, and I'm lost. It's like the last couple of years didn't happen. Everyone else in the room disappears as our eyes speak to each other. The feelings, emotions, and damage all come to the surface. I feel it before I can help it. Squirt looks up and must see it too because she starts to yell for Shadow, Tink, Rebel, Glory, Raven, and whomever else. I don't hear it because I'm fading fast. The last thing I remember before it goes completely dark is my mom calling my name, as my dad is yelling for someone to catch me. Then those powerful arms wrap around me as I go under, though his unique scent reaches my nose before all else disappears. I take a whiff and know I'm totally fucked. My Malty is here. For good or bad, he's here.

EIGHT
'MALCOLM'
MALTY

All hell breaks loose as I try to hold on to Frankie. Just when I lean down to catch her, my back locks while I'm bent over, and now, I'm afraid I'm going to drop both of us to the ground. Well, until a huge guy with long brown hair rushes toward us, and at the last minute somehow manages to grab Frankie and keep his body close to mine so I don't collapse to the floor. He gently hands Frankie to another man, who is also huge. He looks like ex-military from what I can see. The first dude literally shuffles me to one of the couches off to the side of the stage. He leans down, grabbing a few pillows then gently pushes me down onto the couch, adjusting the pillows. Before I can say a word, the other dude also carefully places Frankie on the other couch. She's totally out and if my body hadn't betrayed me, I would check on her. For Christ's sake, I'm a damn doctor who's useless at the moment.

"Hey, don't worry, she'll be fine. Frankie's a fighter.

I'm Avalanche and that one over there is Noodles. His ol' lady is Tink and my brother, Panther, unfortunately is with crazy-ass Shadow. We are just one fucked-up family, dude. Nice to meet ya, though not under these circumstances. Let me go grab both of ya a water, hang tight."

He turns to go, I guess get us some water, when yet another man with long black hair that is braided down the center of his back walks over to us. He gives Avalanche a look then comes by me, crouching in front of me. He pushes a water bottle my way.

"Drink some of this. You're probably dehydrated from traveling. All the stress and worrying isn't helping. Hey, look at me, umm, Malcolm, right? I'm Panther and they will take care of their sister, no worries. What's wrong with your back? Why'd it lock up like that, you didn't even have her entire weight? No, we all saw you almost go down, so for us to help you we need to know what we're dealing with. Do you need a doctor? We can call Dr. Cora to come take a look at you. She's at the ranch but it wouldn't be a problem. Just say the word, brother."

My head is spinning as every single person I've met has been open, friendly, and wanting to help without knowing our story. *Frankie couldn't have landed in a better place,* I'm thinking. She found her chosen family and by the looks of it they adopted her as well. I hear a slight moan and glance around both Panther, and now Avalanche, who's come back with two more bottles of water to see some of the women with the vest things on standing, sitting, and kneeling around Frankie. The scary one with the skull on her face is checking her pulse. Damn, is she in the medical field? Didn't think people in Montana would be so open-minded to have a doctor who looked like her. Though gotta say, that tat is phenomenal.

"Nope, Malcolm, my Nizhoni is not a physician. In fact, she's on the exact opposite of that spectrum. Oh sorry, Nizhoni is Navajo for beautiful. And Zoey, well most call her Shadow, is my woman and the Devil's Handmaidens Motorcycle Club enforcer. So if you put that together, she does more damage than healing; though those she works over deserve that and a hell of a lot more. What do you know about the club your Wildcat is involved in?"

I shake my head. How the hell did she get the nickname Wildcat? I have a million and one questions but don't know where to start. Panther pushes up and then takes a seat next to me. Avalanche pulls a chair over just as the other man, think his name is Noodles, also grabs a chair. All three just sit and wait like they have all day. I drink some more water as I watch both Billie and Enzo sit on either side of Frankie. She's come to but seems disoriented, which is understandable. Michael is sitting on the arm of the couch right next to me. I see Avalanche look his way, and it dawns on me no one has introduced my friend to anyone.

"Thanks, guys. Before I ask the million and one questions I have, this guy here has saved my life so many times I can't even count them. This is my best friend and brother, Michael. Michael, this is Panther, Avalanche, and I believe Noodles. Panther is with Shadow, who's Frankie's club's enforcer. Noodles is with Tink, the prez, and Avalanche seems to be like you… single."

Michael snorts then gives a smirk to each of the men. *Oh shit, please don't start any shit*, I think to myself. Michael generally has issues when meeting new men. It's always something like "No, my dick is bigger than yours. My balls hang lower than yours." He's a great guy though doesn't play well in the sandbox. Before he says a word, Avalanche leans closer to both of us, pushing his long brown hair out of his face. Then his eyes lock on Michael's.

"Nice to meet you, Michael. Just fair warning, not sure what you do in New York but out here we treat our women like the queens they are. Even the ones we aren't involved with or just sleeping with. The Devil's Handmaidens Motorcycle Club might be a one-percent club but they are also women, as you can see. Oh, that means live free, ride free, and die free, if you didn't know. They don't follow any rules but their own. Their mission is to save victims from human trafficking, domestic abuse, and whatever else assholes in this world are doing. They take the victims out of the situation, take them to Tink's ranch, and with time and a lot of help turn them into survivors. Hey, no judgment here, but I saw the looks you were shooting at some of the women. Though I don't know your history, I will tell you this, brother, fuck with any of them and you will have an army come down on you. Malcolm, not sure what your boy's problem is with women, especially Wildcat by his looks, but he better control it. She's gone through enough and now that her past is knocking on her door, she needs support not drama."

With that, Avalanche gets up and walks over to a few of the Devil's Handmaidens sisters. They quietly talk amongst themselves as I turn to glare at Michael. *What is his problem?* I think to myself. He didn't have to come, no one asked him to. Well, Billie kind of did but think she's regretting it now. I'm glad Avalanche called him out because now I know to watch him around Frankie. Come to think about it, he's never been her biggest fan. Gonna have to have a talk with my boy, see where his head is, because if this goes right, Frankie will be my woman again.

Enzo and Billie are helping Frankie up and as much as I want to join them right now, my back is still cramping up. I look to Panther, who studies me for a second or two, then gets up, walking to Frankie and her family. He has some words with them and they turn and walk down a hallway.

"They are going to get Frankie into one of the offices so she can lie down. Her mom is Billie, right? She said if you want to try and talk to her you can, but they aren't leaving her alone. That's your choice, Malcolm. The problem we have is whatever happened in both of your pasts is coming back into Frankie's present. And from the little I've been told; it's emerging back into your path also. Might want to think about sharing whatever it is.

No, I'm not pressuring you, just giving some friendly advice. Life is a circle and if you don't follow your path, you will fall outside of said circle and never achieve your full worth on Mother Earth. So do you want some ice for that back of yours, or are you going to attempt to hobble your way down to the room Frankie is resting in? Your choice, though my Nizhoni generally doesn't like to see her sisters in distress, so don't take too long to decide."

I feel Michael's eyes on me so I look his way. I catch it before he can hide it, a glare pointed at Panther. Okay, what the fuck now? Have I missed something about him all these years? I mean, he's a very successful businessman. And has always been there when I needed him. Well, except when we were attacked, he could not be found. He finally showed up a day or so later while I was in a coma, or that's what Enzo told me. Something pops in my head but before I can retrieve that thought, it's gone. Son of a bitch, what am I missing?

"Mal, my brother you came all this way to finish this off. If you want to go down there and talk, between all of us we'll get you there. Remember, it's up to her though to let you in and accept what's gone down. Now, you two definitely need to talk and don't forget Frankie can be uptight so don't get discouraged, just make sure you're prepared if it goes south. I got your back, brother, always."

Something about that doesn't sit right. When I look to the two men sitting with us, I see they must feel the same way by the intense looks on their faces. Noodles is watching Michael very intensely, while Panther seems to be doing some sort of meditating or something. When he opens his dark as hell eyes it's like he sees right into Michael's soul, which has even him leaning away from the man. I've had enough, for Christ's sake.

"Dude, not sure what's going on or what the obvious problem is, but knock it off, Michael. You of all the people here know what I went through when Frankie left. Well, left after I pushed her away. This is on me not her, don't forget that. Now if I can get a hand up, think I'm going to make my way down that hall after I hit the bathroom. Can one of you direct me to a restroom, please? Oh, and I'll take some ice if it isn't too much of a bother. Thank you."

Panther and Noodles immediately stand and with one on each side, they lift me like I weigh nothing. Then when I'm stable, Panther leans closer to me.

"Come on, my friend, I'll show you were there's a bathroom. You can freshen up too. I know for sure these bathrooms are stocked with everything you could need. I'll wait, no don't rush on my account, but when you're ready I'll go with you to see Frankie in the back office. Noodles will get you some ice. I'm feeling you could use a friend in the room with you since, apparently, her folks won't leave you two alone for whatever reasons."

I can feel the anger coming off Michael from Panther's friend's comment. Before I can turn his way, he gets off the couch and stomps to the door and out. Panther looks to Avalanche. The big man stands and makes his way to the door also. How do they do that? It's like they can talk without words.

"Yeah, that's right, Malcolm, we can. The Navajo people believe that some are blessed with powers or whatever you want to call it. Avalanche and I are brothers, though not of blood. We grew up on the reservation together and when old enough we entered the military together. We were taken as POWs and the only way we could communicate mostly was through our empathic ways. I thank the Great Spirit for that because we each had days that without the other, we wouldn't have made it through. I know that sounds strange, as from what I've been told you are a physician. Keep an open mind, that's all I can tell you. Now let's get you down the hall. The restroom is going to be on your left. I'll be right outside the door if you need anything. Noodles is going to make his way down to where Frankie is, to let her parents know you are on your way, after he gets your ice. We've got your back, friend."

For some reason this kindness from strangers has me feeling very emotional. There is no judgment or bias, just them being beyond kind. Panther guides me to the bathroom where I take care of business. Then I wash my hands, throw water on my face, and breathe. Not sure how this is going to play out, but one thing I'm sure of is, my Frankie has been taken care of here with these people. I don't detect any prejudice or ill will from any of them. They are actually a Heinz fifty-seven of all kinds of folks. It's very welcoming and not judgmental like New York is.

When I've taken some time to gather my thoughts, and more importantly my emotions, I open the door to see not only Panther but Avalanche waiting for me. The look on Avalanche's face tells me something is wrong.

"Is it Frankie, Avalanche?"

He shakes his head slowly at first, not meeting my eyes.

"No, Malcolm, it's your friend Michael. Apparently, he has issues with me, or more importantly, my heritage or maybe my skin color, who the hell knows? Which surprises me because, no disrespect intended, but I'm sure you both have come across prejudices throughout your life because of your skin color. He refused to even talk to me, told me he'd rather talk to Noodles. So I came back and sent my brother out to try and settle him down. Don't worry, nothing is going to happen to him. We are all allowed our opinions and as we both say, we can agree to disagree. We're all educated adults who don't have to always be on the same page, right? Now, let's get ya to your woman."

"No, she's not my woman, Avalanche. I blew that after what happened. I was so deep in my own pain that I snapped at the one person who meant the world to me. I'm here to try and put an end to what started back on the day at that cabin."

"Don't be blind, brother. If you didn't matter, do you think Wildcat would have passed out from just seeing and hearing your voice? She didn't do that until she saw

YOU, not her mother or father. You, Malcolm. Keep that thought up there in your head when you talk with her."

We all just look at each other for a minute or two, then Panther turns, and with me squeezed between them, we make our way down the hallway to a section that shows a few doors, probably the different offices these men spoke about. Well, it's now or never. Time to man up and admit I was wrong. I can only hope Frankie will open her heart to me and not only listen to me but also believe and forgive me.

NINE
'WILDCAT'
FRANKIE

My fucking head is killing me. I know Mom and Dad mean well but I'm not a kid anymore, they have to quit trying to baby me. Yeah, didn't mean to pass out but besides the utter surprise of them both being here, I've not eaten today. We're shorthanded here at Wooden Spirits, so I've been trying to help wherever I can. Now I'm sitting in one of the back offices we use more for a quiet place for employees to chill and maybe eat their lunches. It has a small love seat and a few tables with two chairs at each table. Right now, I'm on the love seat with Mom and Dad each in a chair they pulled close to me. No one is saying a word, but I can tell they want to, they're just too damn afraid. That's on me. I didn't handle this whole shitty situation right. I mean from when we were attacked at the cabin and all the time from then to now. Probably shouldn't have run away and only called a couple times a month. I can't even fathom what I put my family through, not knowing where I was. Guess it's time to put my big girl panties on and act like the adult I keep saying I am.

"Hey, guys, come on, it's all okay. I was just a bit shocked and think my sugars dropped too. Haven't had a chance to eat today, we had one server out sick and are still shorthanded. Sorry to scare you both. Now, how did you find me? No, I'm not mad at all, it's great to see you both. I've missed you like crazy. How are my crazy-ass siblings doing? I haven't spoken to any of them recently. Last time I think Shamonda told me Pepe was deployed again and she was ready to have that baby. Is she doing okay?"

Mom and Dad look at each other before my dad replies.

"Yeah, honey, she's fine. Her and the boys are spending time at Malcolm's to watch his cats, along with Buddy and Chloe."

They both are watching me closely so they see how the name of our dogs affects me. That tore my already bleeding heart out when I left home. We rescued both of them. Buddy was going to be used as a bait dog as whoever had him filed his canine teeth down. They were probably going to either use Chloe as a bait dog too, or maybe breed her though she was a collie-something mix. They were crazy together and hated loud noises. When Mal started to get the cats then everything changed in our lives. I need to know before I face him again.

"Umm, well, guess I should ask because no one has told me differently, is Mal married or at least have a significant other? Any kids or other fur babies I don't know of? He looks good, so can I assume he had a full recovery?"

Mom glances at Dad and I brace because I know that look. The "Billie" look, not the usual Mom look.

"Frankie, why don't you ask him those questions? Daughter of my heart, it is time to quit fucking around…"

Dad and I both gasp. Mom might cuss but the "F" word very rarely comes out of her mouth. Damn!!!

"Yeah, I used that awful word but you need to know how serious all this shit is. And, no, he didn't have a full recovery but that's his story to tell. I think it's about time the two of you…"

Mom stops as a knock on the door interrupts her. Before any of us can say another word, the door opens and Avalanche is in the doorway. I can see others behind him but unsure who it is.

"Hey, Shorty, you doing okay? If so, got someone who wants to make sure you're okay. Maybe have a word, if you're up to it?"

For some reason Avalanche had taken to calling me Shorty, which makes sense. I'm all of five feet four-ish and he's like a foot or so taller. I give him a small smile and nod. He moves into the room and behind him is Panther then Mal, who looks scared to death. Slowly, so I don't hit the floor again, I stand and make my way past the two large men to stand in front of Mal. He looks down at me and all the feelings I've had for him rush me. Before I can think about what I'm about to do, I reach up and wrap my arms around him. He doesn't hesitate to do the same and, like before, Mal always gives the best hugs. He wraps his entire body around you so you feel surrounded by him and safe. We stay like that for a bit then, reluctantly, I let go and move back.

"Hey, Frankie, good to see you awake. Are you okay? Do you have some time? I'd like to talk with you."

Looking around, it seems like no one is planning on getting up and leaving, so I wave my hand for him to follow me. I take one end of the love seat while Mal takes the other side. We both sit with our backs to the arms of the piece of furniture, so we are facing each other. Mom and Dad moved their chairs back so now they are sitting in line with Avalanche and Panther. All four are introducing themselves, so I take a moment and look over at Malcolm. He's beyond gorgeous. He's doing the exact same thing to me.

"You cut your beautiful hair. I mean you look sassy as shit with that cut and your curls are so bouncy. Finally liking them, huh? And, wow, tattoos, didn't see that coming. Not sure how to do this, Frankie, but shit, how'd you end up in Timber-Ghost Montana from New York? And more important, part of a motorcycle club? Cop to member of a club, you have to explain that to me."

I shake my head to try and clear it. Still don't know why they are here so I throw that out first. Before I can say a word, Noodles walks in with a bag of ice, which he hands over to Malcolm. He leans forward and places the ice against the love seat arm then leans onto the ice.

The small moan tells me it feels good. What's that about?

"Sure, Mal, we can catch up but first, can you tell me why you are here after all this time? I mean, if you truly wanted to find me you could have, so I'm guessing something is up. So spill it, Malty. And first, what's with the ice? Did you get hurt trying to save me from cracking my head open?"

His eyes shoot to mine and I cover my mouth. Damn, that's what I used to call him when we were together. Not sure how it came about but at times it fit him, and other times it broke that guard he tried to keep up. From the corner of my eye, I see my mom get up and approach us. I look back at Mal and he looks so serious. I find out why seconds later.

"Frankie, I'm sorry that I must bring this to you, but damn, I can't believe all this shit went down and it was just yesterday. I was working my shift in the emergency room when I heard a voice from the past. No, don't panic, let me finish. It was that jagbag, Gerald. The crazy as shit one. I think he was the boss of the assholes who showed up at the cabin that day. Or maybe not, there was that huge guy also. Anyway, I didn't want him to know I was there but, as usual, my plans went to hell because he went crazy and attacked my boss, Judy, so I jumped in to tried to protect her best I could. When he saw me, his crazy went to epic proportions. He started spouting out about how it was time to take care of the two loose ends that fucked his life up. He mentioned the other guy, Joey, but didn't elaborate. Once I got home, I called your folks to fill them in, and that's when you called to say someone was out here looking for you. We decided with that information it was time to finish this chapter in our lives. And here we are. Oh, Gerald is in police custody as he's in prison. Had a bad fight with another inmate, that's why he ended up in the ER. Now it's your turn to share and tell us your story."

I gulp then hiccup. My nerves always give me away lately. I glance at my parents and Panther with Avalanche. The big man gives me a serious look but his eyes as always are twinkling. Looking at Avalanche, I wonder why I never took a chance and went down the road with that tall, dark-haired, handsome man. I know why and right now he's taking a seat next to me, his knee touching mine. I've never gotten over Malcolm Washington. Now, as they say, a door is opening and it's up to me to either walk through it or slam it shut. I know deep inside I'd never shut him out totally, so I take a deep breath, sit back in the love seat, and gather my thoughts. This has been a long time coming.

"Well, not sure about you, but I've been in therapy on and off since what happened at the cabin. Once I was almost healed, I went back to the force but it wasn't the same. I seemed to always be scared of my own shadow. You were out of the coma but still in the hospital, so my plan was to try and get as close to back to normal as possible, so that when you got out of either the hospital or rehabilitation center, we could move forward. That ended because of two reasons. First, I was getting some weird phone calls and shit left at our apartment, at the station, and on my car. My sergeant knew about it but not many others. Yeah, I know, Mom, I didn't tell you or Dad, didn't want to worry you. Then you told me in that horrific and nasty way to *'get the hell outta your life.'* After about the third or fourth time, Michael was in the hallway when I burst out of your room. He told me it would be best for both of us—no, all involved—if I just stopped coming around because you had so much healing and recovery in front of you that me hanging around nagging and bringing you down wasn't helping. He even offered me money to start somewhere else. No, I didn't take that jagoff's money, though I did crack him in the face for offering. Not sure you know, Malty, but he and I never really liked each other or got along. And that was on him. I truly tried because I knew he was your best friend. So I packed up what I had and the night before I was going to head out I got a call, telling me my 'dark ass' better move along or else. No, it wasn't Michael or anyone I'd have met with the two of you. The voice sounded crazy as shit, but there was an underlying threat there. He and, yeah, it was a man who didn't like a woman of color for sure. Told me what 'my type' was good for. Like cleaning houses, spreading my legs, and pushing out kids. That scared me because, if you remember back to the cabin, those guys kept saying how after they were done with us, they'd be accepted in as they passed the final test. That has bothered me over the years. I always thought maybe a hate cult of some kind.

"Anyway, I spoke to one of my friends who told me out West was beautiful, so I took a chance. By the time I got out here to Montana, I was a shell of myself. Guess PTSD had set in. I was afraid of every dark spot or loud voice or noise. I'd not healed from the trauma but didn't want anyone to touch me. I needed a job so when I was driving through all these small towns in each western state, I kept looking for something I could do under the radar. I fell into Timber-Ghost, Montana and that's where the Wooden Spirits Bar and Grill was looking for help. I applied and Tink hired me on the spot. After a couple of months, I was approached by Glory to prospect in the Devil's Handmaidens Motorcycle Club. I liked the thought of a 'chosen family,' though not sure I'd fit being different. Well, let me tell you, besides you, Mom, and Dad, along with my siblings, these women are my heart and soul. I got through prospecting and once I became a member and got my patch and rocker—these things on my kutte. The club, who owns the bar and grill, offered me the position of manager of both. That included a hike in my pay, a very generous benefit package, but more importantly a build up to my confidence of being able to do a good job. After I left New York and my job, I felt like less than nothing and at times still do. Though my therapist from the Blue Sky Sanctuary helps me deal with those feelings and thoughts."

I take a minute or two, then keep going because if I'm putting myself out there I'm going all the way.

"Now, in regard to dealing with what happened to us, I've been trying to do more of that. Saying that, with the club's mission being trying to save victims from human trafficking and domestic abuse and rape, it has forced the issue. I honestly don't know all that was done to me as I was unconscious from the vicious beating I took. And for that I thank the powers that be, and yeah, Mom, God too. I do know how and what I felt after when I woke up in the hospital. Not sure about you, Malty, but my personal life has been lonely. Saying that, I have tried to move forward, but nothing or no one has given me any type of incentive to try and put the work in."

I glance at Avalanche, who's watching me intently. I know why I never pursued him. He's too good of a friend—no, brother—to lose that for anything else. And my heart still belongs to Malty, though he didn't seem to want it back in the day. I hear a growl and look back at Malty. He's glaring at Avalanche, who just shoots him his good ol' boy smile.

"There something you need to share, Frankie? Do you and that huge mountain of a man got something going on?"

Before I can respond, Avalanche lets a cough out before he busts into laughter, hitting his thigh and everything. Panther looks at him like he lost his mind. So do my parents. That is until he drops a bomb.

"*Malty*, the difference between you and me is if that fine-ass woman was in my life and bed there would be no fuckin' way I'd let her go, no matter what happened or where my head was. And that's the damn truth. Now, I'm thinkin' y'all need some time alone, so my brother and I are going to go out and aggravate the women. Sir, ma'am, very nice to meet you. Hope to see you around. Oh, and, Malcolm, just some advice. Get your head outta your ass before this woman replaces you with someone who can handle all of her. I get bad shit happens, believe me I do, but don't let it ruin your entire life, brother. Look at what's right in front of you."

With that, Avalanche and Panther stand, walk toward me, pulling me up. First one then the other hugs me tightly, with Avalanche whispering he'll always be there for me and how he loves his little Shorty. Once they are gone, my parents stand and hug me and Malcolm before walking out the door. I look to Malcolm, who looks to me and all I can do is wait and see where we go from here.

TEN
'RAVEN'
BRENNA

Fuck, never thought I'd be doing this shit again. Poor Freak, he's dying over there, got some kind of sinus thing going on. Thank Christ I have an air purifier in my office because I can't afford to get sick. Ash and his family are getting ready to shift their herds from one pasture to another, so me getting sick almost guarantees that he will too. The Sterling family can't have him go down and end up in bed, so I've upped all of my vitamins and am drinking orange and apple juice.

From the little information we were able to get from Malcolm and Wildcat's family, along with the photo Squirt took of the asshole looking for our sister, Freak was able to kind of get a pattern on him. Oh shit, we know his name is Joseph/Joey McKallen. He was living in New York then New Jersey. From what I can see, he's been in and out of trouble just about all his life. After the incident with Wildcat and Malcolm, he kind of pulled up roots and disappeared before they could arrest him like

Gerald. Left behind a few women with kids from him without a thought. I'm thinking they are all better off. Though he continued to stay in touch with Gerald, the guy who ended up in the emergency room that Malcolm ran into. Gerald even placed some collect calls to Joey a few times from prison. Though he never attempted to visit, as there has been an active warrant out for Joseph McKallen since the attack at the cabin. One man died from the shot from Wildcat and another, besides Joey, got away, though neither Wildcat nor Malcolm caught a name. He was one of the men who brutally assaulted both though.

Taking a minute, I walk over to the mini fridge and pull out two waters. Then I reach in the cabinet above and grab two packages of Emergen-C, which is something that is supposed to up your immune support when compromised by illness and stress. I've been giving it to Freak for the past eighteen to twenty hours and he's not gotten any worse.

"Raven, found something. Yeah, can I get another one of those? I feel better since I've been drinking that shit. So look at this. Joey has been in and out of town for the past three weeks. He's been to the Wooden Spirits, the trucking company Devil's on Wheels, and even checked out your gym. Before you ask, I hacked into all the computers. If you didn't know his past by the way he acted, you'd think he was a decent guy. He went into the grocery store a few times and even flirted with the cashiers and shot the shit with Bernie, the butcher. Fuck, I'm gonna start cracking up again. How Bernie became the butcher is hilarious. So long story short, this Joey is making the rounds. Establishing a presence. He was at the bank and bakery too. Oh, and stopped at the garage shop to buy some shit for his truck. I've got model and make, along with the plates, though they are stolen, just saying. I'm not sure if the truck is, would need the VIN number for that. Whatcha think he's up to?"

After all I've seen since I became a Devil's Handmaiden and all of our investigations into human trafficking, I figure he's trying to integrate into the town to keep suspicion off of him.

"We need to know where he's staying. Have you checked all the abandoned Thunder Cloud Knuckle Brotherhood locations? From what Malcolm and Wildcat have told us, this group of men was very racist. During the attack at the cabin, Malcolm heard them telling him they were going to beat his colored ass then string him up the way he should be. Gerald accused him of trying to take jobs and work from his brothers, like Joey and the other guy whose name we don't know. The sadist of the group. If they are prejudice and racist, what's to say they don't know the brotherhood or are hoping to be a part of it. I'm guessing, brother, but what else can we do at this point?"

"Good thought, Raven. I know that Panther and his group, including Dallas and Chicago, had put up some remote cameras on the properties your club busted up, along with that area where the Grimm Wolves club blew up that compound. Give me a few minutes. Hey, would you mind grabbing us something to eat? I'm fuckin' starving. Oh, gotta run to the can. I'll work on this once I get back."

He jumps up and rushes to the bathroom across the room. That's my clue to get the hell out of Dodge before he erupts. I've worked way too long with Freak not to know what just happened is his way of telling me he's got to take a dump. And just saying his bathroom breaks always need time to air out. Thank God there's a fan, hey, I don't hear it. Dumbass.

"Freak, turn the damn fan on, for Christ's sake. This room isn't big enough for the both of us and what you're doing in there. Gonna run to the kitchen, see if any of the sisters started lunch. Be back shortly."

As I walk out of my office, I hear him cackling in the bathroom. I've gotten to know Freak well as we work closely together a lot. He's got a good heart and works like a dog until he finds what he's looking for. As I come out of the office, I'm surprised by the number of people in the great room of the clubhouse. Not only my club sisters but also Panther, Avalanche, Dallas, and Chicago. They are talking with Tank, Enforcer, and Yoggie. I give a nod here and there until Tank pulls me close, giving me a side hug. Gotta love this big teddy bear. For a brief second, we thought we were gonna lose him, but he fought back and is stronger now than ever.

"How's it goin' back there, Raven? Freak pulling his weight?"

"Yeah, he is, Tank. Thanks for lending him to us yet again. Without him, I'd go friggin' crazy for sure. I'm on my way to find us some food."

He gives me a squeeze then lets me go. As I walk toward the kitchen, it hits me that Wildcat and her man, Malcolm, aren't around. I'm hoping and praying they both get their shit together 'cause they are perfect for each other. I know, even though the other sisters don't, Wildcat has been working with Sheriff George and Yoggie to maybe become a deputy for Timber-Ghost. I had to do some inventive let's say legal/illegal shit to make her legal but not use her full name. Didn't know why when I did it, per Tink, but now I do. She's been on the run all this time. For fuck's sake, what is wrong with people?

I push open the door as the smell of something heavenly reaches my nose. Heartbreaker is putting her famous chopped salad together as Dottie is at the stove frying something in a pan and she has two big pots steaming. One, I'm assuming is her sauce, and two, some kind of pasta. Dot loves to cook up some Italian food. I move toward her and literally scare the shit out of her when I lean around her to see what she's frying. Oh man, I want one now. She made her famous meatballs that have a center of cheese, peppers, and garlic. I glance around and see a bunch on a paper towel, so I reach for one. She pushes me with her hip.

"Don't you dare, Raven. I'm busting my ass to cook, don't go stealing my balls. Maybe try some manners and ask before you just reach around me. What the fuck, sister?"

I can tell something's crawled up her ass. I turn to Heartbreaker, who's watching the two of us. This sister has been struggling for a while now. Since she fucked up her sobriety and went back on drugs. When Tink was looking for Hannah, Heartbreaker had an idea where she was but the drugs were more important. I think she's made her amends, but shit, who am I to even assume? I do remember Shadow taking a round at her and Heartbreaker has the scars to show. That's one human being, and I use those words lightly, who I wouldn't want to wake up to. Shadow could scare someone to death, I'm sure. Heartbreaker mouths "Michael" and it all makes sense. That's Wildcat's man's friend, and he's a total dog and player. I hope to Christ he didn't fuck around with Dottie 'cause that will just piss Wildcat off. And like her name, that's something you don't want to do.

"Dottie, would it be possible to get two plates for Freak and me? I'd appreciate it, we've been holed up in my office now for hours and we're both starving."

I give her, what Ash says are my puppy dog eyes. She just sighs and looks over me to Heartbreaker, who's already putting together two to-go bowls of her chopped salad. Gotta love that sister, for sure. Dottie reaches above her to get two huge to-go containers and starts to fill them up with pasta, sauce, and meatballs on top. Then she grabs the shredder and puts Parmesan cheese on both. Damn, my mouth is watering.

After I thank both of my sisters, I pick up the containers and grab some silverware. Making my way out, I glance around and see Wildcat's parents sitting off to the side taking everything in. Just as I go toward them, Tank looks up, sees where I'm looking, and gives me a chin lift. Then his group walks over and starts to introduce themselves. Awesome, now I can get back to my office and eat this food while it's hot. If the room doesn't smell like an outhouse at a campsite. Freak needs to talk to Dr. Cora about his bowels. Something ain't right. When I get to my office the door is cracked open, so I push on it and see Freak is done and it smells good in the office. He's set the small table off to the side. He comes to me, grabbing the containers and bowls. As we work together getting our lunch set up, I wonder why he doesn't have an ol' lady. He's decent-looking when he cleans up, though on the thin side. He's probably at genius level and generally he's a good guy. Wish I had someone to set him up with, but whichever club sisters are single wouldn't want to get the two clubs mixed up like that. I mean, already we have Taz with Enforcer and Glory with Yoggie from the Intruders. All I can do is hope someday a woman comes along who will treat Freak the way he should be.

"Fuck, check this out, Raven. My alarms just went off on that facial recognition software Ironside shared with us. It's Joey and, damn girl, you hit it right on the head. He's at that compound where Shadow's dad used to hide out. And from the looks of it, he ain't alone. I thought your prez said that crazy as fuck group of losers were gone from around here. If so, who the hell are all of those folks?"

I look at the camera he hacked into and am shocked at all the people walking around that compound.

Goddamn it, this shit is never gonna end. That brotherhood is so friggin' huge. Well, before anything, I'm going to eat then I'll reach out to Tink and Glory. See what they want us to do. The scary thing is why is this Joey, who's asking around about Wildcat, hanging out with the assholes who associate with the loser club the Thunder Cloud Knuckle Brotherhood? That will be something my prez will want to know. Kind of makes sense because of the way he treated Wildcat and Malcolm at the cabin. He was brutal and from what I've heard, insulted both of them because of their heritage. What a dick, but hey, most are who hang around with that bunch.

In a matter of minutes Freak and I are sitting at the table, enjoying the first meal we've had in like almost a full day. Neither of us is speaking, just shoveling the food in as fast as we can. It tastes heavenly.

ELEVEN
'WILDCAT'
FRANKIE

We both have taken a seat across from one another. He hasn't said a word, so I assume it's going to be up to me to start this long-awaited conversation.

"Why, Malty? For what reason did you not want me around anymore? To do what you did, I hope you know you broke me more than those animals ever could. Is that why you couldn't think of touching me again after what they did? It took me all this time to start to trust and believe in myself. Hours, weeks, months of therapy, not only because of the brutality but also because of your harsh and emotionless words, time and time again. Even hurting, I sat by your bedside, day in and day out, while you were in a coma. Do you have any idea what they did to me, Malcolm? Well, let me tell you. I was ripped from front to back. They penetrated me not only with themselves but they used something else to cause as much damage as possible. And they succeeded, as I was torn to pieces. I woke up in the hospital in so much pain my screaming woke me up. The doctors were giving me pain medication but didn't want to give too much that would keep me from waking up. Eventually, I had to have surgery to correct a fistula that occurred during my rape, probably because I was gang raped or that's what the doctors thought by the DNA they found in and on me. And just so you know, I never once blamed you for anything. I loved you, Malcolm, and when I needed you most, you pushed me away, again and again. I tried to talk myself into trying to understand that you were in excruciating pain, but damn it, so was I.

"When you finally woke from the coma, I thought we were both on the way to mending, at least physically. By the time I was able to attempt to go back to work, I was given desk duty as I didn't even try to pass my physical to go back out on the streets. I was mentally and emotionally scarred, and terrified at the thought of being out there by myself. And being on the desk, my hours were regular so I could keep a schedule to be there for you. Though that wasn't what you wanted, was it? You wanted Michael, your best friend, but you didn't want your fiancée to be around or help you. Do you know he got even meaner to me the more you pushed me away? Even my parents started to worry when he was around. I bet they weren't happy when you showed up at their door with that bastard with you. Yeah, that's what I think of him. When you were at your lowest and needed people around you, he pushed all of us away. I wondered if he was the one telling you to push me away.

That you didn't need me or my problems. For the first time I got a taste of what hate was. It was directed at him first, then I began to detest you. For being so damn hateful and cold-blooded. It felt like you were acting like you were the only one injured. Don't look at me that way. I know they also assaulted and raped you. Do you think I'm stupid or was an idiot back then? Malcolm, I saw that asshole behind you with your jeans around your ankles, the look of devastation and utter pain on your face. Why do you think I came out to begin with? I shot and killed one of them. It's my fault I didn't act quick enough to prevent them from hurting you. My God, don't you know I've been carrying this guilt around since that moment? You never looked at me the same and it's because I saw. Yeah, Malcolm, I saw that maniac raping you."

Tears start to fall from down my cheeks but our eyes never lose connection. I can see all the emotions in his eyes before his shoulders start to shake. I remain in my seat and as hard as it is I don't reach out to him; in fear he'll push me away yet again. When his eyes fill up, I bite my lip so hard I taste blood. It is when his hands reach for me that a gasp escapes my lips, and we both stand from our chairs and fall into each other. Not sure which of us sobs harder, though it isn't a contest. This was the aftereffects of mental, physical, and emotional rape, along with post-traumatic stress.

I'm not sure how long we hold on to each other. Malcolm shuffles us to the love seat and we fall into it, never letting each other go. Neither of us says anything.

What can we say that will heal either of us? Even though this happened in our past, neither Malcolm nor I have dealt with the aftermath of that day. I will never go to a cabin in the woods for the rest of my life, no matter what. Just going to Raven and Ash's wedding on the Sterling ranch was hard enough. I need to reach out to my therapist and start getting real serious about trying to work on these issues. Life is passing me by and the more I don't work on them, the more those deranged assholes win. They've taken enough from me already. And from Malcolm.

I lean back and look up at him. Those gorgeous eyes are more bluish-green today. He lifts his hand and lets his fingers wipe away my tears. I do the same for him. When he leans down, I'm unsure but shouldn't be. He places a tender gentle kiss on my lips then pulls away.

"Frankie, first, my God, thank you for sharing. I never knew the extent of your injuries. I asked but seemed like no one wanted to give me any details. Shit, I need a second or two please. You don't know everything from my perspective and I want—no, need—to share that with you. Is there a bathroom close by? I need to well, got to take care of something, and then clean my face and get a towel to clean you up too. No, let me do that for you."

He's not telling me something, so I point to the small bathroom across the room. He pushes himself up but I can tell he's either in physical pain or something is bothering him. Takes him a moment to walk to the bathroom and close the door. Leaning back, I don't move, just try to calm myself from everything I just told Malcolm. Shit, I can't believe that, in the matter of under an hour, I shared with Malcolm stuff that even to this day my own family doesn't know. My therapist has been pushing me to open up to my family. She even said pick just one person and explain to them what happened. I explained I'm still ashamed, you know, being a cop—even a new one—and not being able to protect Malcolm or myself. The guilt has been eating away at my soul. My therapist finally got through to me when she brought to my attention it was me against four men that I know of.

Suddenly, an overwhelming smell sneaks into the room. My God, what the fuck is that? Immediately, I get up and open the only window behind my desk. Not wanting to embarrass Malcolm, I softly knock on the door.

"Malcolm, I'm going to go get some coffee. You still drink it, right? I'll be right back."

I hear him mutter a "yeah" before I walk out the door and down the hallway. When I enter the main room it's still pretty full with people. My eyes are drawn to my parents, who both stand and start to walk my way. We meet halfway and I grab on to both of them.

"I'm so sorry for pulling away. No, really, as crazy as it sounds, in a way I'm glad this is happening. We need to arrange some time while you are here for me to share some things with you two. It's long overdue. First though, I need to get some coffee for Malcolm and me."

"Frankie, make sure its decaffeinated for Malcolm.

Don't think his gut can take regular coffee. He never drinks it at our house."

I look first at my dad then my mom. *Why can't he drink coffee?* I think to myself but I don't ask. That's up to Malcolm to explain, and I'm done putting my parents on the spot.

I kiss them both then walk right to the kitchen. I pull out one of the carafes we keep for our chapels. I move to the industrial coffee machine and set it up for a pot of decaffeinated coffee. While it's being made, I grab a tray and place some cream and sugar on it. On the counter are some fresh homemade cookies, so I add them to the tray. When everything is ready, I carry the tray through the main room and down the hall to my office. The door is wide open so I walk in to see Malcolm on the love seat, elbows to his knees, hands in his hair.

I put the tray on the table, turn, and close the door. Then I take a seat next to him but don't touch him. The odor is gone but I can smell some air freshener. The window is still open.

"Ready for some coffee, Malcolm? Mom and Dad told me to make decaffeinated, so I did. Still like cream and a ton of sugar?"

When he glances up at me, I'm shocked at how devastated he looks. On instinct, I lean into him. He puts his arm around me and just holds me close. Neither of us says anything, probably too afraid whatever is said will ruin this moment. After about five or so minutes he leans down again, putting a soft kiss on my head.

"Yeah, Frankie, could use some coffee. Are those

cookies sitting on that tray? So I see you still have a need for sweets? Grab me a cookie or two before you demolish them, being the Cookie Monster that you are."

Just that sentence reminds me of back in the day when we didn't have a care in the world. I'm not sure what the future holds for the two of us, but if it means I can at least have Malcolm as a friend again, I'll take it. Though I want to be selfish and want more. I want everything.

TWELVE
'MALCOLM'
MALTY

Watching Frankie get us both coffee; it dawns on me at this moment that this is it. Time for me to step up to the plate, as they say. I owe it not only to her but also myself. It's been a long goddamn time coming. All the pain we've both been through changed our lives forever. My biggest fear right now is, once she hears what happened and all I've gone through, she won't want me in her life in any way. Not sure that we even have a chance to maybe pick up or start over, but just having her in my life in some way is vital to my well-being now that I've seen her.

I'm so deep in thought, I jump when the coffee mugs hit the table. Shit, what the hell is wrong with me? Frankie has a cookie in each hand, waiting on me to pick one. Instead of just one, I reach up with both hands and grab each one before she can pull her hands back. The look on her face is priceless. Reminds me of happier and more carefree times. After we both eat two cookies and sit back into the love seat to drink our coffee, I look anywhere but at Frankie. That is until I feel her hand squeezing mine. When I look her way, she gives me a small, sad smile.

"Malty, no matter what you tell me, it won't change a thing. We both went through a living hell, but they didn't win. We are both alive and though fucked up, they didn't achieve what they wanted. Good prevailed somehow. Now take your time, we got all the time in the world, Malcolm."

Feeling her eyes on me warms me to my soul. Takes away the cold dread of what's to come. This isn't going to be easy at all, but maybe getting this shit off my chest will give me a reason to truly live, or at least try. So many things are going through my mind and as minutes go by Frankie never says a word, she just holds my hand. Finally, when I feel I might be able to get through this, I clear my throat while squeezing her hand.

"I'm not going to rehash everything, as we were both there. I'll tell you what I remember. When I pushed you into the cabin and locked the door, I felt such release that the beating they put on me didn't even faze me. Well, the goddamn pain did, but in my mind I prayed that if I didn't fight back, by the time they'd killed me help would arrive, and you would be saved. Naïve to say the least. When I heard them talking about how my kind deserved everything I was going to get from them, I knew this was going to be the worst of the worst. When the big guy grabbed his crotch with that maniac look in his eyes, I knew that this was going to be pure torture and probably like being in hell on earth, and guess what, I was right. I kind of remember the three of them beating me until I was almost unconscious, then as the two of them laughed the real fun was going to start. Frankie, I've never told anyone what happened. The long and short of it was they took turns going at me. You came out toward the end of it when they were trying to hang me. Gerald, the asshole, and the guy you shot were talking, not realizing that I was hearing them. The asshole said this is the way the country should be and my kind didn't have a place in the USA. Or maybe an option for my people is to do all the menial jobs because we ain't smart enough for anything else. Gerald said something about me being in medical school and he thought he heard us talking about you being done with the police academy. That told me they were around before we got there to hear us talking, unless they were stalking us before. We'll never know."

Taking a big gulp of lukewarm coffee, I roll my shoulders and crack my neck. Then I dive right back in.

"I wasn't going to go down without fighting. One of them went to the far side of the cabin, hearing you screaming. He was banking on you wanting to help. Right before you came out, Gerald got a couple of good kicks to my back before they pulled me up, rope around my neck. You saved my life, Frankie, though not worth the cost you paid. I fell and landed on my back, which immediately I knew by the amount of pain something had happened. I couldn't feel my legs. I was in and out of consciousness when the asshole came back, flipped me over, and violated me with some sort of object. Not sure what as I passed out. The next thing I remember is waking up with you by my side in a hospital gown. When I was told how long I was out, couldn't believe it. When the doctors told me what they were planning, I knew I wasn't going to hold you back or ruin your chances at a future, no matter what that was going to be. Something just hit me. What you told me, you're right. Michael was all for me pushing you away. They were going to take a part of my bowel and there was a chance that I would end up with a colostomy bag, though they didn't know if it was temporary or permanent. After you left, I wasn't even going to have the surgery, just wanted to die. The decision was taken from me when I went septic. They once again induced me into a coma and removed a section of my bowel and put in a colostomy bag. You probably don't have a clue what that means, so it's the bag you wear on your stomach that collects stool. I was lucky they were able to reverse it about three to four months later after my colon had healed. I've gone through similar procedures a couple more times. The problem is every time I go through a surgery the side effects become more prominent. A perfect example is when I had to use the restroom. I don't have the control and it's a fifty-fifty shot if I'll be able to hold it in, so I try not to take any chances. That doesn't always work and, yeah, I've had accidents over the years. In the beginning, after they reversed the colostomy bag, I could cough or sneeze and I'd shit my pants. I started wearing Depends, just for the in case times."

This time when I reach for my coffee, Frankie stands and goes to grab the carafe then refills both of our mugs. I can see steam so know this is going to taste a lot better than that barely warm coffee. When Frankie sits down this time, she parks it right next to me. She leans into me and I breathe in her scent. Goddamn, I've missed her fresh, fruity smell. Together we just sit close, her waiting for me to continue and me trying to get the guts up to finish the story.

"After the third surgery, I figured my life was always going to be one surgery more. This time though, the specialist who I was seeing wanted to try something different. Man, was I frigging beyond happy when she told me that all the damaged bowel and intestines had been removed, and as long as I follow the rules that I should be able to live a full and almost normal life. That got me thinking, so I worked on getting as healthy as possible. Then I finished my residency and took the boards. I was always interested in the emergency room so when an opening was posted, I applied and got it, end of story. Then Gerald showed up in my ER and opened the door to our past. Fast forward to right now. I'm sitting next to you after all these years and even with reliving the past, I wouldn't change a thing, Frankie. I've missed you, Beautiful."

I watch her eyes dilate and her breath getting short, coming in and out quickly. Even with the discussion we just had I can feel my cock filling out and lengthening. My God, I can't remember having this kind of a reaction with anyone else, ever. I watch her eyes go right down to my jean-clad crotch. I watch as she unconsciously licks her bottom lip. That has precum covering the head of my dick. Damn it. This is not the time for this, there are too many things we need to hash over before we even consider taking this huge step, if we ever get to that moment again. And both of our heads must be on the same page.

"The reason I had to run off to the bathroom is I'm having some issues and probably will need another surgery soon. Best way to describe what's going on is, have you heard of Crohn's disease or ulcerative colitis? I never been diagnosed with either but the way my body is acting is mimicking them. If I have the surgery, will probably need to have a stoma opening again and temporarily have a colostomy bag. Last operation it took two months for my body to be able to heal and then adjust back to the normal process of taking a shit. Damn, that sounded gross as hell, sorry, Frankie. So to say I was shocked to see Gerald in that room and to hear what he was spewing rattled me enough to put my hurt feelings aside and call your parents."

I hear her gasp so I look down at her to see first her eyes go big, then just like my old Frankie, her cheeks flush and the sparkle appears in her eyes. Fuck, not sure why she's pissed, but it's so damn good to see she didn't lose her spirit.

"Um, Malcolm, your hurt feelings? Maybe you are having a lapse in judgment or memory, but you pushed me away, not the other way around."

Well, we are here. Guess if I'm baring my soul, better just put it out there.

"Yeah, Frankie, I pushed and pushed but that last time I told you to go you did go and without a fight. You left me in a hospital bed with who knew how many upcoming surgeries, or if I'd ever have a normal life. That's where my hurt feelings come from. I'm not saying it's your or my fault, it's just the hand life dealt us. It sucks and has since you left. I swear to Christ, just sitting next to you it's like the colors in front of my eyes are brighter and clearer. You give that to me, Beautiful."

I see them before they flow over. Never do I want to make her cry, but I'm thinking these are cleansing tears that are so overdue and needed. Maybe what everyone has told me is true: life is a journey or circle. We are trying to deal with all that happened to us and only the powers above know what's next for us. I do know I'm going to change, no matter what, because I want Frankie to be a part of my life, bottom line. Just as I go to tell her that, the door bursts opens and there is Michael standing there, face flushed, hands in fists, his eyes finding mine first, then shifting to Frankie's. I know whatever he's about to say is going to piss me off for sure. Though before a word comes out of his mouth, I hear boots on the floor then a few of Frankie's sisters come into view with Noodles, Panther, and Avalanche. It's Panther who walks directly behind Michael and seems to press on the side of his neck before my best friend even realizes what's happening. With stunned eyes, I watch as

Michael collapses and Panther gently puts him to the floor.

One of Frankie's club sisters steps over him, letting her foot graze him hard on his side. *Wow, what the hell?* I think to myself before she changes the rest of our day.

"Wildcat, you both need to follow me to my office at the clubhouse. Freak and I discovered something you need to see. And this prick is going to Shadow's wet room because once we show you what we found, you just might want our enforcer to do what she does best. Get rid of the trash.

THIRTEEN
'WILDCAT'
FRANKIE

Not sure what the hell is going on but I watch as Avalanche leans down and picks Michael up like a sack of potatoes, throwing him over his shoulder. Then both he and Panther head down to Shadow's wet room. Damn, I pray this is a mistake because I don't think Michael will be able to survive a session with our enforcer.

Raven wastes no time getting back to her office. Inside it's a disaster, paper and laptops and tablets on every available surface. Freak is at the side table, fingers pounding probably over a hundred words a minute as fast as his digits are moving. Raven points to two chairs that are facing her desk. Her computers are facing the chairs. She leans back against her desk, legs crossed. It's like she's waiting for something and she confirms that when she looks our way.

"Waiting on Tink, Glory, and Shadow. This is way

over my pay grade. Sorry, sister. All I can tell you is to brace."

The hair on the back of my neck starts to stand up as tingles go down my spine. When I turn to Malcolm, his eyes are back on Freak. I mean the man is a genius with technology, but damn, a shower and brush might help him. And maybe a few dozen meals. Malcolm must feel my eyes because his lift to mine. I give him wide eyes and he does the same right back at me.

"Are they going to hurt Michael, Frankie? I'm not sure what's going on, but if you have any say so, tell them not to hurt him. He grew up rough and didn't have a good family life. Still doesn't barely have any contact with them. That's why he kind of gravitated toward my family. All of us kids were given grief for being mixed. With Dad being black and Mom white, it wasn't easy for us, though we had each other. My parents kind of adopted Michael, though not legally. He ended up spending more time at our home than his own. Later when we both graduated and I went to college, as you know, and he put some time in the military. On one of his leaves my dad kind of let it slip that back in the day he was handing money over to Michael's folks so he could stay with us. I thought Michael's head was going to burst off his shoulders. He accused my parents of buying him, which was so far from the truth it wasn't funny. They understood he was hurt and angry so they let it go when he later apologized. It wasn't too long after, Dad shared his family's home burnt down with his parents trapped inside. Everyone thought it was a tragic accident, but now I'm not too sure. Fuck, I'm going to have to let my parents and siblings know about him if what I think is happening happens. Son of a bitch, I trusted that jagoff. Damn it, Frankie, I'm so sorry I brought him into our lives."

I can't imagine what Malcolm is feeling. I don't think, before my Devil's Handmaidens sisters, I have ever had a close friend like he had with Michael. Malcolm considered him like one of his brothers. Fuck, if that asshole is somehow involved in any way this will devastate Malcolm. I do know Raven wouldn't call in our prez, vice prez, and enforcer if she didn't find something substantial. Before I can even comprehend where my thoughts are going or what I just revealed to myself, the door to the office opens and Tink and Glory walk in, shutting the door behind them. Freak starts gathering the stuff off the table, putting it on the floor next to him. Raven moves around to her desk as both women take a seat on the two other chairs from the table that are up against their wall. They pull them closer to Malcolm and me. I can see the looks they are giving him, so I figure better speak up.

"Tink, Glory, this is Malcolm my fiancé. He was with me at the cabin that day I kind of told you about. Before you say a word, we've already worked out some of what happened and I'll explain later. Where is Shadow? Please don't tell me she already started in on Michael. We don't know that he has any involvement in whatever is going on. Both Malcolm and Michael have been friends since when we were all in high school. Can you call Shadow, tell her to hold off until Raven explains what she found? Please, Tink? Malcolm doesn't understand any of this and it's moving way too fast for both of us. Plus, my parents are here and I don't want them to get the wrong idea about our club. Again, I don't ever ask for anything. Please, Maggie."

Tink has been watching me and with me using her given name her eyes shoot to Glory, our VP immediately reaches for her phone from inside her kutte. I hear her whispering then disconnecting.

"Caught her just in time. She had pliers to his toenails but she said she'd put him on ice. I reminded her to not do it literally, and she gave me her crazy laugh. Best I can do, Tink, without going down there and pulling her out of her playroom, as she likes to call it."

Malcolm looks between the three of us before running his hands over his face.

"Frankie, what the hell is going on? What kind of people are you associating with? Was this Shadow about to murder Michael? My God, what the fuck is this? I feel like I'm in an alternate universe in the middle of Nowhere, Montana. This can't be happening."

Tink stands up and walks to Malcolm. He goes to stand and she places a hand gently on his shoulder. I know that look on her face, have seen it way too many times when we are breaking up a human trafficking circuit and she's pulling the victims out of their own hell. Malcolm glances at me and I just give him a small nod.

"Malcolm, I know you're confused, so maybe if I explain a little this will make sense. I know how you feel, no, give me a chance, please. Then you can have the floor. Over twenty years ago, I was violently raped and got pregnant. With the help of my parents, who honored my choice to keep my baby even at that young age, I did just that—and had a healthy little girl. Then they took over taking my daughter, Hannah, and raising her as theirs and she became my sister. Sounds crazy but it worked for us. Until one day when we were at the park and someone kidnapped her. She was lost to us for many years. I vowed to find her and I finally did, with the help of all the women in the Devil's Handmaidens club. Our mission is to break up human trafficking groups or as they are called circuits. Then we bring the victims to the ranch and help them reacclimate back into society after their traumatic event. Some move on or go back to family. Others prefer to stay here with us and work the ranch because they feel safe here. Now, before you say anything, give us about five more minutes because I'm going to turn this over to Raven to explain what's she found out. Well, her and Freak, who's part of my dad's club. Patience, my friend."

I turn to Malcolm, grabbing both of his hands and squeezing. His eyes shoot to mine and I can see the confusion, fear, and sadness. I lean over and whisper in his ear to trust us. He pulls free and places his hands on my face. I see when he decides to do just that before he nods. Then we turn back to Raven, who now has Freak next to her rocking on his feet. Dude needs to stop the energy drinks before he has a heart attack or stroke. Raven looks to Tink and Glory first. Then she glances at Freak before her eyes rest on us.

"Okay, if anything we say doesn't make sense just stop us, and we will go over it again. Malcolm, before we start, just so you know, Freak and I have been doing this for years. We're good at what we do so if we tell you something, believe me, we've gone over the facts and researched them, even going to the dark web to make sure we're correct. In our business lives are at stake. Okay. When Squirt, well Hannah, told us about Joey and shared that photo, I immediately started to dig into his past. At first it wasn't anything alarming. Then I hit on something, so after talking to Tink, we pulled in Freak because he has a special skill set that is different than mine. I found out Joey had connections to a racist group that has, I guess you could call them chapters throughout the United States. We've had contact with this group. They are bad people, Malcolm. The kind of folks who judge people on their race, color, religion, or even if they are 'different' than the norm or what they consider normal. I personally know how insane they are. I was kidnapped, beaten, and when cornered, shot last year by one of them. He knew there was no way out so he wanted to do the most damage before his death. Freak started going through their lists of members. Now their members are throughout each state, and are men and women who have either the financial background to get what they want or might have something the Thunder Cloud Knuckle Brotherhood needs to further their cause. Now I'm going to let Freak tell you what he found, please just keep your mind open. Go ahead, brother."

I squeeze Malcolm's hand and he returns it and hangs on to my hand. I know it was hard for Raven to talk about the attack and she minimized her injury, as she almost died. Well, she flatlined at the scene and on the way to the hospital. Her recovery was hell on both her and Ash. I can't believe they have come so far from that point in their lives. Movement catches my eyes as Freak moves a computer screen so he can push a large one facing us. I gasp as picture upon picture appears on the monitor. All of them have one thing in common. Michael is in them meeting different people in what looks like different locations. Now, at first most people assume Michael is black, but he's Puerto Rican. Or that's what his mother has said. Both of his folks have substance abuse issues and didn't give a fuck about him. That's why Malcolm kind of adopted him and so did the Washington family. If this is going the way I think it is, then it will affect all of Malcolm's family. Freak wakes up another laptop and starts pounding away on it.

"All right, when I saw the picture from Squirt something stood out on Joey. The tattoo on his left forearm, so I researched that design. We've seen it on other members of the brotherhood. As I was digging further, started to see photos of men who didn't match up with the Thunder Cloud Knuckle Brotherhood MO. Turns out they have been reaching out to different minority males who have had rough lives. They convince them that together they can change the world, or some bullshit like that. I'm not a person of color who's come up in the world being treated worse than dog shit, so I don't get why a person would, one, trust them, or two, want to join them. Maybe you can get an answer out of Michael. Hang on, Malcolm, I'm getting to that. You must have known how bad his family life was with his parents. Well, guess at one of their lowest moments they offered their young son to the brotherhood to run errands and erase their own debt. And the rest is history. As Michael aged, his involvement with that bunch got deeper. I know he just about lived with you, did you notice anything different about him when you guys were around fifteen or sixteen? He was a suspect in a double murder, where two white women were raped and brutally beaten to death. From what we can gather that was some kind of initiation."

Malcolm pulls his hand to his lap while shaking his head violently.

"No, that's not possible. How would we not know any of that? My parents treated him like one of their own. I mean, we were as close as two kids could be. How the fuck didn't we know? If he was a suspect, why didn't the police come to our house and ask questions?"

"Because, Malcolm, even though you truly treated him like family, he wasn't, and had his own fucked-up family. The police questioned his parents, who provided him with an alibi. It wasn't but a month later that the fire happened. No proof, but from the evidence out there I don't doubt Michael murdered his parents—maybe with help, maybe not—and started the fire. He's beyond damaged, not only by his sick-as-fuck parents but also by the many years he's been a part of the brotherhood. Did you know Michael knows both Gerald and Joey?"

I feel Malcolm jerk back as if someone punched him right in the face. Now I wish Glory wouldn't have called Shadow to step down from working Michael over. That motherfucker deserves everything she would have done to him and more. I don't have a good feeling about this at all. When I came to in the hospital, I remember the first time Michael came to my room to "check in" on me. I didn't understand the smirk on his face, but I was in so much pain and the drugs messed with my head. Since he knew Joey and Gerald, I wonder. Oh God was he a part of our attack? Holy shit did he rape me? And if so, why?

Malcolm jumps to his feet, the chair falling backward. He goes to turn but I grab him, holding on tightly, knowing it's coming. When the cry comes from his chest, it sounds like an animal in pain. Then comes the shaking fits and finally the sobs. I see everyone get up and leave except Raven. She comes around her desk and hugs me from behind. She gets it because she's been through something very similar. This is how my parents find us and they don't say a word, just wrap the three of us in their arms as Malcolm cries from the depths of his broken soul.

FOURTEEN
'SHADOW'
ZOEY

Not sure how much longer I'm going to be able to calmly sit here with this jackass smirking at me. Something about this piece of shit makes me think I should know him, and in my profession, I always trust my gut. I'm racking my brain to try and fit his face, though I don't even know what I'm trying to do. When I hear a dark chuckle, I look at his face. This time it's me smirking. I might not be torturing him but he's not going anywhere either. He's on the specialized piece of wood that I had one of the guys from the sanctuary make for me. It's just wide enough to hold someone's waist against the width of it, but the arms and legs hang off the sides, which makes it very convenient to hang small weights off the wrists and ankles. My thought behind this type of torture is it's slow and extremely ball-busting painful. I should know, I designed the wood table pole, and the weights depend on if the person is in good shape or bad. What eventually happens to the asshole on the table is their shoulders can't handle the weight and they dislocate out of the sockets. This jagbag, Michael, I've got to give him some quiet kudos. Since I put the additional weight on a few minutes ago, not at any time since I started adding weights has he shown any sign of pain. I know he's experiencing it, even though he's trying to be as stoic as he can manage. Actually, as time goes by, it's starting to fucking piss me off.

"So guess you don't recognize me, do you?"

My head snaps back before I can control it. First thing a person must do in this type of situation is control all movement and emotions. Don't engage because then they have the upper hand. I know this, goddamn it, why did I react? So at this moment I decide if he keeps running his mouth, I'll use duct tape to keep his pie hole closed. Then my world shifts.

"Do they call you Shadow because of that thing on your face? Or is it because you move like a shadow in the night? Come on, tell me, Shadow, or should I call you by your real name? If I remember correctly, it's Zoey, right? Zoey De Luca, the daughter of Dario De Luca? He was your father, right? Is any of this coming back to you, *bicha*? How about that cage remember how he kept you in it and only took you out for you to entertain his new friends?" The deeper rumbling sound of his voice immediately has my guard come up as goose bumps form on both of my arms. The baby hairs on the back of my neck are standing up. A reel of film starts rolling in my mind's eye and I can't stop it. Holy mother of God, no, this can't be happening? Not now. Fuck no. Then he starts to laugh and I lose it. My eyes skim the area until I find what I want. Moving like my name, I grab a six-inch Gordon Bowie knife in one hand and brass knuckles in the other. Michael is grinning like a lunatic as I approach him. His next words literally eradicate my soul.

"Do what you have to, Zoey, but you will never erase me from your thoughts or more importantly your nightmares. You and me are connected in so many ways, bicha slut. The way you obeyed me every single time I visited Dario, if not you paid because there are always consequences with your actions. Remember how I pounded that into your head literally. I'm sure you remember what bicha in Puerto Rican means right? Well, it appears at this present time our roles are reversed. Or are they? Let's see if you can give as good as I gave you back then."

I raise the hand with my Bowie and swing down across his chest. I'm not going super deep, just enough to make it burn. This is not going to be a one and done, it needs to last. I've done this enough my entire life in the Devil's Handmaidens so that I could do this all day and still he wouldn't die. Back and forth I find my rhythm and just keep at it. Blood is covering my front and Michael isn't laughing anymore, which is a good thing. So caught up in my never-ending nightmare, thanks to my dad, I never hear the door behind me open or my name being yelled out. One minute I'm swinging and the next I'm up against the wall. Fuck, wrong thing to do as I push off while swinging my body to the left then right to break away. I know deep down this person has no intention of hurting me. What they don't realize is my mind—no, my entire being—is back there in my past, not here in the present. I turn my body and swing my hand with the brass knuckles into their side. A solid kidney punch and whoever it is goes down with a hard thump. Fuck, when I see the red hair I know instantly it's Heartbreaker. *Goddamn it,* I think as I fling the knuckles off my hand and drop the knife.

Poor Heartbreaker is in agony. I can tell by the sounds coming out of her. It was a direct hit to her kidneys. Fuck, I need help immediately or my sister could die. I walk to the table and dial Goldilocks.

"Kind of busy, Zoey."

"Got a situation, one of our sisters is hurt. Need someone down here now. Michael is in some trouble also. I totally fucked up. I'll explain when you get down here."

I disconnect before she can ask her million and one questions, as usual. Yeah, I fucked up and not only that, I hurt a fellow sister. That's my main thought as I kneel next to Heartbreaker. When I glance up at Michael, he's still grinning as blood drips from every cut puddling on the cement floor below him. I don't give a damn about him. My concern is for my sister. The door to my wet room flies open with Raven, Rebel first, then Tink and Glory. Wildcat is behind them with Malcolm close by. When he sees his friend cut and bleeding, I watch him approach him, not thinking at all. Jumping up, I get between them, hands on Malcolm who tries to shrug me off.

"What the hell is wrong with you, Shadow? My God, he needs to get to a hospital. Help me get him down."

"Not gonna happen and he's far from dying. Believe me, Malcolm, if I wanted him dead, he'd be fucking dead. Malcolm, you don't know who this monster is so you need to relax and let me explain a few things to you about your friend, Michael."

Raven is on one side of Malcolm while Rebel is on the other, making sure the situation doesn't go south, I get that, though this time I made it go that way. Glancing around, I see Goldilocks/Tink watching me. I give her a head nod to the door and she understands. Just as I'm about to walk out, Michael starts screaming.

"Zoey, don't go. Come on, we were just getting started. I'm sure you've had years to think about me in your nightmares. Come on, slut, if this is the best torture you got then you didn't learn a thing from me years ago. Don't quit on me now, you filthy biker *bicha*."

The room goes deadly quiet until Wildcat grabs a towel out of a cabinet and walks over to Michael, who has gone instantly quiet when she approaches. She stuffs the towel in his mouth, turns to Malcolm, and mouths, "I'm so sorry, Malty." His head drops as we walk out the door.

"Zoey, you know him? How? What's wrong? Come on, talk to me. I'm here. Please, you're scaring me. TALK TO ME, ZOEY, GODDAMN IT."

I look down and into her stunning green eyes filled

with worry. It doesn't matter anymore; everyone knows what happened to me.

"Michael is the worst kind of sadist. I belonged to him for almost a year before Dario demanded I be returned back to him. I thought he was either dead or found a hole to hide in. Goldilocks, I'm sorry. You said not to touch him, but when he started poking at me, I just totally lost it. Had to poke him back and make it hurt. He's not going to die but he's gonna be in some severe pain. And shit, Heartbreaker, is she okay?"

"Hey, don't worry, we got this. Now take a few breaths, then we're going back in there and you're going to tell us exactly what, when, and how you know Michael. 'Kay?"

I nod as I lean against the hallway wall. My head is pounding and my insides are flipping all over. Dario and his demented ways and the choices he made for me will never go away. I'll never be free. No matter how hard I work at being a better human being. No, not better, just a human being.

* * *

One minute I'm covered in blood, looking at the faces of my club sisters, the next I'm wrapped up in arms around my waist. Wildcat is holding on tightly.

"Shadow, don't let this sick prick win. I don't know what he's been spewing to get in your head, but remember, like all of you have been telling me; whatever happened is in the past and you've moved forward.

You've already won, sister, not him. His life is shallow and without love, friends, family, or anything that is important. I don't care what he was a part of, look at him now. It's all an act, he's petrified and knows he doesn't have his asshole 'friends' to take his back. Those type of people, especially men, need to have others around to feel strong and in control of every situation. He's being controlled by you and you alone. I don't care if you kill him but make him suffer like he's never suffered before. Please, sister, do that for me and I'll owe you for the rest of my life. I'm not leaving but I don't have that in me, wish I did because with him it would be a pleasure. Like a once in a lifetime moment."

Looking down at my sister, who just had her past blow back and blast her, the fact she can worry about me speaks highly of who Wildcat is. No wonder she was on to being a great cop, she has the instincts. Need to talk to my dad, get him to fast-track her application. Timber-Ghost could use another good deputy. Maybe Wildcat and Yogi can pair up. Fuck, who would have thought two patched members from our clubs would end up on the police force. Life sure the hell plays some wicked games.

"Thanks, sister, you're right. I'll let him squirm in it, though his shit brought back a ton of things I've tried to forget. I will put him to ground but first, I think you and Malcolm should have your questions answered. Especially your man, sister, because he looks like he's losing his right arm which, in a way, he is. That motherfucker was so good that even Malcolm didn't see the evil lying right below the surface. Let me get cleaned up and have a word with Goldilocks and Glory. Not sure, but my ass might be in some serious trouble. I ignored my prez's command and went rogue. There are always consequences to my actions. Please tell Malcolm I didn't mean to disrespect him or you. To me, that jagoff, Michael, is as evil if not worse than my father Dario was. They walked in the same circles. Wildcat, don't believe his lies because he's had years to become the heinous human being he currently is. Something is seriously wrong with him because I know what he's part of, and I know he had a hand in what happened to the both of you. We'll talk soon, but for now, let's take a break from all of this. I'm getting the stink eye from Goldilocks, so gonna see what's got her looking at me like a crazy tiny lunatic."

I squeeze Wildcat's hands then walk toward the one person who saved my life so many years ago. It's been a while since I've lost control, and I can see the concern in Goldilocks's eyes. I mean, she's seen me at my most manic and insane moments to where I am right now. Sure, she doesn't want to see me take steps back. Fuck, neither do I. When I reach her, she is instantly in my space, arms around my waist. Damn, didn't think I was so huggable, for Christ's sake. But if I had to admit it, her tiny arms feel good right now.

"Don't play badass, Zoey, I can see your fear and worry, you can't hide from me. Please give it to me straight, how bad is it that we have Michael here? I can call Dad, Enforcer, and Wrench to get rid of him if you want me to. They'll make him suffer as much as you want. Don't let the dark pull you back, Zoey. I can't lose you, neither can the club. Not to mention your new life including Panther, Avalanche, and the guys at the ranch."

I've loved this tiny person since the first time she stuck up for me in that field years ago. She managed something no one else ever has in my entire life. Well, except Panther. She has a place in my heart because she's never let me down. Always has given me all her trust and support. Her worry and concern brought me back from where Michael was trying to drag me back to. I lean down and give her a kiss on the cheek, which has her jerking back. Yeah, I know, I'm not one who does all the touchy-feely shit. That would be tree-hugging, crystal-loving sister Taz, of course.

"Love you, Goldilocks. Always have and will 'til the last breath I take. Thank you for just being you. I won't let him win but for Wildcat, Malcolm, and me, it's got to be me who puts him to ground. Saying that, let's let him simmer a bit. I'll have Rebel work him over a bit, but don't want him dead yet. I get the feeling he has way too much needed information in his noggin about Dario and the Thunder Cloud Knuckle Brotherhood, along with the circuits associated with both. I thought Raven said she had a lead on a domestic situation or a small circuit of some kind between here and Bozeman, if I'm not mistaken. Once she gets the information, we'll have to move fast on it, so put that asshole on ice. Only water, no food or just the minimum to keep him alive. Limited options to speak either ball gag, rag, or tape. Keep his discomfort at peak levels. Whoever is left behind has to be someone who can fuck with someone or we get Enforcer or Wrench over here. With that said, are we good, Maggie? I know I fucked up and I'm sorry, Prez."

Her head jerks all the way back. Can't remember the last time I called her Maggie. The worry in her eyes turns her green eyes to an emerald pine tree color. She reaches up and grabs my cheeks.

"To you, Zoey, I'll always be Goldilocks. That's just ours. Or Prez, but never Maggie. When you use that name, I know you're pulling away and that I won't ever accept. You hear me, you badass motherfucker?"

That has me laughing out loud. Tiny and mighty. Maggie-Goldilocks-Tink is one of a kind. Talk about badass. She just told me in her no uncertain way that I'm all good and so are we. I give her a nod then walk back into the room and over to where Michael is still on my unique wood table ledge. Malcolm has checked out his cuts and even stitch three of the bad ones. I'm not gonna ride his ass 'cause he doesn't get this at all. Michael's eyes follow my every move. They get huge when I pull out a bottle of booze. He knows what I'm about to do because he's done the same thing to me and probably close to a hundred other women after he whipped us raw then, as he would say, he had to clean the marks we made him give us. So with that thought in my head, I open the bottle, walk over, and before Malcolm can grab my hand, I pour the liquor over all the cuts, small and large. Michael tries to scream but the rag keeps most of the noise down. When I pour the alcohol over the deepest one, I see his eyes roll and then he passes out. Or he wants us to think he did. I don't give a fuck and when I look to Malcolm, he stares at me for a moment then shakes his head. I see Wildcat come up behind him, grabbing his hand and pulling him so he turns, and they both walk out the door, never looking back at this asshole.

Me, on the other hand, I reach out and grab his balls, squeezing tightly until I hear the sound I want. A choking sound has me lifting my eyes to his, which are shooting flames my way.

"This is the prequel, Michael. There will come a time when you won't be able to talk or even moan your wish for death. That's when the real fun begins. I'm not doing this alone. Wildcat and Malcolm will help, along with Enforcer and Wrench. You might not know who they are, but believe me, you're gonna regret what you became associating with Dario. That I can promise you. Now I've got to go, but here's something to remember me by."

Then I squeeze his sack until his eyes start to bulge out. I give them an even hard press then quickly release. If I continue to do that, eventually cells will rupture and release toxins that will damage his liver and kidneys. That's when the real pain will start. I meant it, he's going to feel such pain he'll scream with agony to take his last breath. Only then will I be able to give Malcolm, Wildcat, and myself some peace when I put him to ground to rot for eternity.

FIFTEEN
'MALCOLM'
MALTY

Sitting in the main room of the Devil's Handmaidens club, I'm beyond confused, pissed off, and hate to admit the last, but scared to death after seeing what Shadow did to Michael. *What the hell is going on?* I keep asking myself. How did we get to this spot when all Frankie's parents and I wanted to do was make sure Frankie was okay? We brought the devil's surrogate to her doorstep. How did Michael even manage to sneak in and come to Montana with us? I mean, since the attack and Frankie's leaving, we've drifted a bit. I mean, nothing like we got in a fight and went our separate ways. Just life getting in the way on my side, or I thought so. I have no idea what Michael has been doing, now that I think about it. It's making sense, as I'm finding out that I don't know who the hell he actually is. None of this is making sense but when I walked into that room and met his eyes, he didn't hide from me anymore. I could see the pits of hell in his glare. Something else too, but he pulled that back before I could make it out. It almost looked like sadness, but that could be me trying to make him appear human.

I'm sitting at a corner table by myself, just watching everyone go about their day. When Enzo and Billie rush through the entrance door, I see their eyes searching until they hit mine. Billie moves like lightning and in no time at all she's in front of me, pulling me to my feet.

"Mal, my God, what the hell is going on? How did us trying to make sure our daughter was safe turn into this nightmare we are living? Is it possible that we just got here and everything blew up? Where is Michael? Is it true? How did no one put two and two together?"

I jump as do Frankie's parents when a voice sounds directly behind them.

"Sorry to startle you, but I overheard what you were saying. No one figured out Michael's, if that's even his name, dark side because he's that good. I promise you that he will not be walking away from here. When I'm done with him, what's left will go to ground. Wildcat, sorry Frankie, will be up in a few minutes. No don't worry, Billie, she's not down there alone with Michael, a few of our sisters stayed down there with her. His days of fucking with her are over. If either of you have questions find me, but to let you all know, Michael is part of my past too, and it's not in a good way either. He's a sadist of the highest level and gets off on other's pain and discomfort. Not just physical pain either, but emotional also. He enjoys playing mind games that lead to physical pain. He always gotten off on it and apparently still does. I need to clean up, but tomorrow maybe we can all get together and talk. We've got a situation we need to take care of, but first we'll answer any questions."

Shadow goes to turn and leave but Enzo grabs her hand, which puts Shadow on guard. He instantly releases her but Billie moves in and not only grabs her hand, but pulls her close. Those ice-blue eyes of hers are watching Frankie's mom wildly. Billie raises her hand, cupping Shadow's tattooed cheek.

"Shadow, my husband and I thank you for what you are doing for our daughter. Not just now, but since she managed to find her way out here to Montana. I don't want to think what would have come of her if she was by herself. Seems like Michael has kept tabs on her and somehow recently found out she was here with you and your club. We were talking and maybe he sent that Joey out here to find Frankie. No, let me finish. We've watched two of our kids, Frankie and Malcolm, slowly start to fade away over the last months and years. Please find out what and why from that monster. Then be sure to slowly destroy him because he must pay for the damage he left behind. We will be in your debt forever."

Billie reaches up and places a kiss on Shadow's cheek. Then she turns, grabs Enzo's hand, and they walk toward the kitchen area. I see Shadow watching Billie with her own hand over where the kiss was placed, shock all over her face. I get up close, which has her shifting to look my way.

"Frankie's parents are as we said back in the day 'da bomb.' They don't believe in violence or cruelty of any kind. That was why it was so hard for them when Frankie went into the police academy. Not because they didn't think she could do it, but because of the demented, disturbed, and deranged elements out there in the real world. Their thoughts, like mine, never went to the prejudices that exist out there. If you have a minute, can you explain what your club's mission is? I want to try and understand. Never thought I'd say this, but I've lived a naïve existence. I never thought Frankie and I were attacked for any other reason than happenchance."

Shadow shakes her head and those ice-blue eyes lock on to my eyes. Then she shocks the shit out of me.

"Malcolm, yeah, I'm sure with Michael hanging around my father that race had something to do with it. But because of the intensity of your attack, this was personal. I'm no psychologist or psychiatrist, but if I was to guess—hang on—I honestly believe Michael wanted you for himself. No, I'm not saying you're gay, though there's nothing wrong if you were. What I'm saying is it's Michael who couldn't accept your relationship with Wildcat. He did everything he could to destroy it and when that didn't work, he waited 'til you were both isolated and made his move. Yeah, he raped Wildcat but if you listen to her tell it, she was totally out. He took his pleasure when he was beating her for stealing you away. His hatred for her showed up all over her body. The rape was an afterthought and he might have been the one who used an object on her. Now your situation is different. He'd been dreaming for years of making you his. So when it finally happened, he lost control and seriously hurt you. But not before the men he was working with tried to hang you. Michael gave up something huge to my father to be able to bring some of my dad's goons with him so he could attack the both of you. I don't think either of you were supposed to walk away from that day alive."

My head jerks up at Shadow's words. Holy shit, she might be right. Now that I think of it, between the beatings and rapes, it went on for hours. When I finally passed out, thought I heard one of them say that if they left us, we'd both just die from exposure, or if they were lucky a hungry animal would wander by. Could Michael be so cold-hearted after all my family and Frankie's did for him? My God, what happened to Michael to turn him into such a cold, heartless monster? I'll probably never know, but at least some of this is starting to make sense.

Shadow turns and walks down the hallway as I lean forward, hands on my forehead, elbows on the table. The headache I started with has increasingly gotten worse. This is so bad and on so many levels. I'm so confused on what to do next. Frankie doesn't need us, that's so apparent. She's replaced her family with a chosen one who's had her back all this time. Even now they are the ones in control. I'm the one to blame for what went down years ago. If only I hadn't fallen for Michael's lies. Shit, I doubt Frankie will ever forgive me because I brought the devil into her life.

The scraping of chairs gets my attention. Frankie,

Enzo, and Billie are gathering around the table with me. All with serious looks on their faces. Leave it to Frankie to jump right in.

"Malty, don't try to take the blame for what that bastard did. None of it is your fault. You didn't make him do any of those awful things he did. I'm thinking it was probably him over the years who was responsible for those 'weird things' that happened to us. I'm sure Shadow will try to get it all out of him but get those thoughts out of your head. We need to talk about what's next. I know, Mom and Dad, you can't stay out here forever. You either, Malty. Jobs, families, and fur babies need you. There has been no word on Joey yet, but Tink's dad, Tank, and his club are going to check out where Shadow's dad was holing up. Some of the cameras show movement so maybe that's where he's holed up. We have a situation getting hot that we might have to move on. Oh shit, let me explain that better. When I joined the Devil's Handmaidens Motorcycle Club, I took an oath to do my best to assist in the rescuing of abused and trafficked women, men, and children. That's how a lot of the situations around Timber-Ghost have been cleared up. We've busted or torn down the circuits, bringing the victims to the ranch where they get physical, mental, and emotional help. Some move on and go back to their prior lives and families, while others decide to stay at the ranch to start a new life. We have partnerships with many professionals to help, depending on what we find on each rescue. Sometimes it might be ten to twenty survivors, while other times it's fifty to one hundred. We've had to form close partnerships with the Blue Sky Sanctuary, which is Raven's brother's place for ex-military trying to recover from traumatic situations. Most of the folks over there are ready to deal with and try to heal and move forward. Also, we have chapters of the DHMC all over the country. The Thunder Head Knuckle Brotherhood is one of the organizations and, yeah, they are huge. We've been concentrating on them lately. Believe it or not, they have affected a few of my club sisters. You are all more than welcome to stick around but as you can see, I'm fine and as safe as possible. Not to mention, I can take care of myself. Not only my cop training but we train constantly at the ranch. Tink and Glory take our safety very seriously. Oh, might as well drop another bomb while we're all together. I'm in the process of applying to be a deputy out here. Shadow's dad, George, is our sheriff and he's desperate for some help. I talked it over with Tink, Glory, and Raven, who did a deep search to see if there was anyone on the dark web looking for me. There wasn't and now that we found out Michael's involvement in our attack, once Joey is caught it should put that time in our lives to bed. So I've just regurgitated enough info to each of you, hope it clarifies everything. Do you have questions, concerns, or anything?"

I look at the one woman I've loved for as long as I can remember. I know she's giving me a way out, but I don't want one. Not sure what's happening or if we even have a chance, but I'm not running away anymore.

I look to see Enzo's eyes on me. The small smirk and barely-there nod tell me he knows where my head is at and what my thoughts are. Thank God I have his support.

"Frankie, I can't speak for your folks but I have a shit ton of vacation time. If it's not a bother, I'd love to stick around for a while. Can't remember the last time I took a day, let alone vacation, away from work. If your club needs it, I can do whatever you're short on. A ranch hand, a cook, or cleaner. I might not be licensed in Montana but I am a doctor in New York. Whatever. What I'm trying to say and not doing a good job of is that I'd like to stay and get to know who you are now, Frankie."

I hear a sniffle to see Billie, of all folks, has tears in her eyes. Then she opens her mouth and ruins it.

"Well, damn it, Malcolm, not sure my mascara is waterproof. Though got to say that was gorgeous and stated so eloquently, son. And to add to Malcolm's request, your dad and I are planning on staying for at least a week or two. It's been way too long, Frankie, so we have time to make up for. You go about your life; we won't get in your way. Actually, we are looking for a Vrbo or something close by so we don't continue to impose on your president or club."

This shocks me because didn't think Montana or Timber-Ghost would be a place Enzo or Billie would ever consider a vacation spot. I watch as Frankie glances at her folks before she looks my way. Then she shrugs her shoulders before getting up, squeezing my shoulder, placing a kiss on my cheek, and then moving to both of her folks and doing the same.

"You're all welcome to stay as long as you like. You're family and I'm glad you came out to check on me. I was wrong to run away, but now I can't leave here. This is my life now. I hope you get that. As much as I love all of you, I can't ever go back to New York. Too many bad memories there for me."

With that, she turns and walks toward the bar area where a bunch of her club sisters are sitting. Feeling eyes on me, I look across the table to her parents. Enzo beats Billie to it.

"Well, Frankie was clear, Malcolm. What are your thoughts on moving to this quaint town, or does the big city hold your heart?"

I grin because that's an easy question to answer.

"Enzo, you should know better. The only thing that's ever held my heart just walked toward the bar. Now, if you will excuse me, need to figure a few things out."

Pushing my chair back, I walk through the room and out the front door. Looking around I see a bunch of bikes, cars, trucks, and then not much. Shit, forgot this is small-town USA not New York City. Guess there's no way I can order an Uber or get a cab. I step off the porch and walk to the far side, which has a beautiful view of the mountains. My God, it's breathtakingly beautiful. So serene, quiet, and beyond stunning. So much so I'm lost to the view in front of me, so caught up in what my eyes are taking in that I don't hear anything until a branch snaps. When I turn, I see Avalanche looking down at me.

"Need something, Malcolm? I'm pretty free for the rest of the day. Actually, came here to try and find something to do."

"Yeah, Avalanche, can you show me around and tell me what's so great about Timber-Ghost and Montana?"

He breaks into a smile and his eyes twinkle.

"So am I to assume you might be calling Timber-Ghost home soon? I sure the fuck hope so, we could use a few more good men in the area. Sure, let's go for a drive and I'll show you around. Though, remember, I'm not from here either so I'll do my best."

With that I follow the big man to his truck and he starts it up, heading away from the clubhouse of the Devil's Handmaidens. I pray this could be a new challenge for me but not sure how many doctors are needed in such a small area. I'll figure something out because if I can manage this, I'm not going to leave Frankie again, no matter how much of a fight it's going to take on my part. Though hoping cleaning stalls doesn't become my new job.

SIXTEEN
'WILDCAT'
FRANKIE

After all that's happened, it's almost refreshing to sit with my sisters and discuss breaking up not a human trafficking circuit but a domestic situation that has gotten out of hand. Raven was able to hack the records of the man in question, Jeffrey Walsh. He's a seven-time abuser but every single time he's been brought up on charges they are eventually dropped or the witnesses disappear. This time he's holed up in a cabin out in the woods and deputies have been out there a few times for wellness checks. From the police reports, there are multiple men with a handful of women and children. One main cabin then some smaller hut-like buildings and a few tents. One deputy said it reminded him of a commune. Early yesterday a couple was out camping when someone attacked them. When the man came to, his girlfriend was gone. He managed to get out of the woods so he could catch a cell signal and call 911.

Sheriff George is here along with Yoggie. Tank is also

here because his daughter, Tink, called him. Apparently, the girl missing is the daughter of one of Tank's longtime friends. William and Tank go way back. William and his wife, Sherrie, are both here also. The boyfriend is in the hospital getting checked out. The sheriff starts with what they know and what the plan is.

"All right, William, Sherrie, you sure ya want to be in here? What I'm gonna say isn't going to be easy to hear."

With wide eyes filled with fear, they both nod. Sheriff George drops his head then sighs.

"Well, from what we can tell and what Kevin told us, he and Cici were hiking and were surprised by a bunch of men. While Kevin tried to fight, he was immediately beaten while Cici was 'played' with, their term. Three men surrounded her, tearing and ripping her clothes off. Kevin tried to get to her but eventually his pain was too much. When he felt hands on his own belt, he went ballistic but that didn't stop the men. Both he and Cici were raped at the same time. That's the last thing Kevin remembers before he lost consciousness. I'm sorry, Sherrie, William, but I promise to find Cici. That's why we have Tank and the Devil's Handmaidens here. This is what the DHMC specialize in. Yoggie is not only an Intruder but also one of my deputies. He'll blend in until he needs to use his star to arrest whoever is in charge. I'm guessing this is part of that domestic thing you have going on, Tink. How do you want to do this?'

Tink looks around until her eyes fall on mine. She tilts her head like she does when she's planning on dropping a bomb.

"Sheriff George, I think it's high time you deputize Wildcat. She's passed all the necessary tests and we could use her going forward in a fuller capacity to bind our world with yours. Between her and Yoggie we'd have the law with us on these missions, and maybe that will alter the turnout of how this ends because they are the law working side by side with our clubs. Two deputies serving Timber-Ghost and its residents."

My head swings between Tink, Sheriff George, and Tink again. Finally, a huge sigh is heard just as Shadow goes to speak. The sheriff raises his hand, shaking his head, and for once Shadow shuts her mouth. *My God, miracles do happen,* I think to myself with a tiny grin.

"Well, Tink, get outta my head. My plan was to speak to Wildcat after this meeting but let's fast forward. If you still want the job, Wildcat, or should I say, Frankie, it's yours with a three-month probation period. You will be working with Yoggie as your partner. The rest we can figure out later. Let me go out to my SUV and grab your deputy bag, which includes a bulletproof vest, a star, and some other shit—I mean stuff—necessary or mandatory for the job."

We all kind of giggle or chuckle at George's slip. And hearing Shadow tell her ol' man that our club's bulletproof vests are probably better than what he's going to give me, adds to the laughter. He turns, gives her the stink eye, and walks out. We all wait until he comes back in with a duffel bag filled with stuff.

"Go through it with your new partner, Yoggie, around. Let me know what else you'll need, Wildcat.

Eventually, to follow protocol, I'll need to run you through some tests but as far as I'm concerned, you are now a deputy of the Sheriff's Department of Timber-Ghost. Welcome, glad to have ya, Frankie."

He comes toward me, hand out. We shake hands as all my club sisters also surround me with congratulations being thrown out there. Off in the far corner I see my parents and Malcolm coming forward. Somehow, they knew about this. First Mom, then Dad, hugs me. Finally, Malcolm comes to me, pulling me close.

"I'm so proud of you, Frankie. You never gave up on yourself or your dreams. Be proud of yourself because you won. Wishing you only the very best life has to offer. You so deserve it, Beautiful."

When he pulls away, I grab his hand and squeeze.

"Malcolm, we need to take some time to talk, okay?"

He nods then moves with my parents, who are following Dani out of the huge conference room at the ranch. Malcolm seems different since he came back from his ride with Avalanche. Not sure why, and I haven't seen Avalanche since then to find out what exactly the two of them did together. I know that their stud ranch is very busy at this time of year so maybe he'll show up later, who knows. Was actually surprised to see him here at all.

"All right, hey, quiet down."

Glory is trying to get everyone's attention, though it isn't working. Finally, we hear something banging and when I look around it's Tink, lifting and slamming a travel mug on one of the tables. Well, it worked. Once she has everyone's attention, she looks my way.

"Congratulations, Wildcat. I know that has been one of your lifelong dreams to be a police officer. Also, after you brought this idea to us, it made sense to have a law enforcement person within our club so when we break up the circuits or domestic disputes, we have documentation and all the necessary legal documents, along with your vest camera."

Everyone once again claps and says congrats. Then Tink gets serious.

"We need to find Cici. The longer they have her, the more damage is being done. Sherrie, William, if you want to step out, I totally understand, but now we are getting down and dirty on all the details. We are shorthanded now with both Taz and Vixen pregnant. Obviously, they can't go with, so they will be holding down the mission from our home base while we tighten our approach. That means members and prospects are gearing up. Also, Tank is going to provide a few of his brothers to help out if needed."

As I listen to my prez, my mind goes to what Cici must be going through. My God, why do we have such monsters on this earth? It doesn't make sense to me. That poor girl will never be the same, and I can relate. My life's path was altered that day. Not that my life is bad but it isn't the one I was born to lead. Or maybe it is and I had to go through everything to become who I am now. I'll never know though, all I can do is keep pushing on to, as Malcolm said, find the best life possible. I know that we need to move fast because every minute that young woman is in the hands of those maniacs, they will continue to literally tear parts of her soul out with every action against her. Not just the sexual but the physical beating and berating does just as much damage. Hearing my name, I look up.

"Sorry, Tink, my mind was spinning. Can you repeat, please?"

"Yeah, Wildcat, we are going to need you with us for a couple of reasons. First, you're a deputy now so that will help if we need to go the legal route, which I doubt these fuckers are going to want to honor. Second, you've experienced what Cici is going through so you might be able to help her in that way. Now if what's going on is too much for you then tell me now before we get down to the particulars. Sorry what, Sherrie?"

We all look to Cici's mom. She's staring directly at me and I feel that look down to my bones. Not sure what she's going to ask, but I'll give it to her straight. She deserves at least that.

"Wildcat, right? What did Tink mean, you've been through what my daughter is experiencing? Do you know who these men are? Is it because of your club that they are here in Timber-Ghost?"

Before I can reply, Raven steps up, tablet in her hands.

"Actually, no, these assholes have been holed up for months. We have six young women who have been reported and there are missing persons cases on each from around the Timber-Ghost area."

"Sherrie, what Tink was talking about is a few years ago back home in New York City. My fiancé and I were enjoying a weekend in a cabin in the woods, until a bunch of men approached and eventually beat both Malcolm and me almost to death before they raped us both continually. Only reason I think we are alive is before they got a hold of me, I used a satellite phone, called 911, and they got rangers out to our location. I've been in and out of therapy since. Left my home and somehow ended up in your town. Then I met Glory and Tink. The rest, as they say, is history. Just remember, you've raised a very strong young woman. No matter what happens she's going to need both of you to be there for her, so if she has to fall or let loose, both of you will hold her up until she can do it on her own. With that said, not going to sugarcoat this, it can't get much worse. That's why we need to move as soon as possible. My main objective is going to be to get Cici out, and I'll do whatever I need to. This isn't our first rodeo. We've gone up against some of the most devious assholes and criminals. We've brought back the victims here to the ranch and helped them become survivors. I hope that helps and answers your question. Now, I've got some folks I need to speak to before we push off."

With that I stand and walk out of the room to find my mom and dad, along with Malcolm, sitting in the hallway. All three stand as I approach.

"Hey, can you guys follow me to my cabin please? Don't have a lot of time but need to explain what's going on."

I don't wait, just walk out and pass the main house to the lane behind it where most of the single sisters live. Mine is number nine, which is newer and larger. I totally love my little home and am so grateful to Tink for allowing me to live here. We don't pay rent, it's part of being a member of the Devil's Handmaidens and it keeps us all close. For those who have moved or gotten married or just found their soulmates, Tink sold them plots of land to build their forever homes on acreage still on her ranch.

Walking up my porch, I look back to see Dad looking around. Mom is right behind me and almost knocks into me when I stop. Malcolm's behind Dad. I lift my hand to the small computer screen under the Nest camera bell. It chimes four times then the door unlocks. Once inside, I again lean over and put in the code for the alarm. We learned the hard way when Tink was going through her shit that no matter how much you think you are safe, you never truly are. So with Panther and his group's assistance, all of the cabins, main house, and bunkhouses are now under surveillance with not only our club but with the Intruders too. Panther's men, Chicago and Jersey, are pretty amazing techies, not to mention some of Ollie's ex-military folks. We are set up for hopefully just about anything.

I put my new duffel bag down and walk to the open kitchen, grab four waters, and walk to the table off to the side. Everyone takes a seat. The quiet is too eerie. I open and drink a quarter of the bottle before I try to explain.

"I know all of you are worried. I do get that, but we

have a situation that my club has to get behind now. Time is of the essence. A young woman has been taken by a few men. They first beat her and her boyfriend then raped them both. The boyfriend passed out and they took her. Her name is Cici and she's only twenty years old. They were hiking. Both are from the Timber-Ghost area. I need you to let me do what I do best. No, don't, please. Mom, if you could, go sit with Cici's parents. You too, Dad, I'm sure they'd appreciate it. Malcolm, I'm going to have you hang with Avalanche and Panther. They are our backup, so they aren't going in with us but won't be that far away. This right here is the difference between a one-percent club and a riding club. We don't follow the rules you all do. We follow our club rules, which lets us do what we do to save as many innocents as possible when a situation comes our way."

"But, Frankie, didn't you just become a deputy? How can you do both be a Devil's Handmaiden and a deputy? Is that even possible?"

I look to Malcolm and I get why he asked, but damn, time is wasting. So I give it to my family straight.

"The deputy thing, Malcolm, is so if a situation arises that having law enforcement there is needed, then I'm a go. Yoggie from the Intruders has been doing this since I came out here and it seems to work. It's going to be a fine line. Yoggie, he puts in his time in town and at events. It's good for townsfolk to see the clubs doing public service. Now I got to get ready. Wait here, I'll just be a few. Then I'll walk you guys to the meeting room and Malcolm we'll get you over to Panther and his team."

With that I get up, walk to my bedroom and directly into my closet. I lean in and switch out my worn jeans for a pair of my riding ones, which are heavier and thicker. I grab my biker boots, shoving my feet inside, and a long-sleeve Henley then my holster. Going to my safe, I put fingers on it and it opens. I snag my Springfield Amory Hellcat. Yeah, one of the reasons I carry it is because it's a Hellcat, just like me. The other and main reason is the accuracy of the gun, and I can handle it. Gun in the holster at my side, in my back holster I put my Sig Sauer. Grabbing my hunting knife, I shove it into the pouch in my boot. Last are my kutte and leather gloves, along with my Louisville Slugger. Going to have a word with Sheriff George to see what weapon is approved by the state of Montana for rural deputies. Hate to have to get used to yet another weapon when I'm able to handle these with ease.

As I walk down the hallway, I hear whispers but as soon as I get to the main open area everyone shuts up. Three sets of eyes bulge out at my appearance. Like I said, not going to hide what I've become. Mom jumps up and comes right to me, opening my kutte. She sees my gun and her face blanches. Dad stands but doesn't do a thing. Malcolm, on the other hand, is standing, fists at his sides.

"Frankie, maybe you should stay back this time. With everything going on…"

"Malcolm, I get how you're feeling, truly I do, but

I've got to go. Need to be there for Cici. Let's move. Time is wasting and Cici is the one paying that price."

Without looking back, I grab my leather off the hook, reach down for the duffel, and head back to the main house—well—first the meeting room so Mom and Dad can comfort Sherrie and William. I see Avalanche approach and I hand off Malcolm to him. Though not before he pulls me close and whispers to me—no, begs me—to be careful and places a gentle kiss on my lips.

Seeing everyone going to the barn off to the side of Tink's ranch house, I follow. One of the prospects lined up all our bikes so they are ready. One of the club vans is also in line. I hear them first, but the Intruders make their way to where Panther and Avalanche are waiting. Tink pulls us in and we quickly go over what we are planning. Taz says a few of her prayers then Glory says a prayer to God for safety and everyone coming home whole, including Cici. Then we all get to our bikes and get ready. When Tink gives the hand signal, we all start up and the sound of pipes is what calms me down. We've done this so many times, hopefully, this one will go as smoothly as all the others. One by one, we leave the barn. I see my parents standing with Cici's folks and when I pass, I lift my hand to them. The fear in my folks' eyes I wish wasn't there, probably why I never shared exactly what I was doing out here. Now need to concentrate on one thing only...getting Cici back home to her family.

SEVENTEEN
'MALCOLM'
MALTY

Got no idea what I'm doing, but no way am I letting Frankie leave me and go alone. Yeah, I get that she's part of the club and they've done this kind of stuff before, but I just have a feeling I need to be close. When I get in the truck with Avalanche and Panther, I am obviously going to sit in the back by a huge black canvas bag. Avalanche tells me to check the bag next to me. When I open it, I can't believe my eyes. It is sort of a medical bag but on steroids. Not sure how they got all this stuff and, personally, I don't want to know.

"You're a doc, so if it comes to it, we wanted you to have whatever you'd need. No, Malcolm, we aren't asking you to break the law or your oath, just to be around in case one of the good ones needs some medical attention."

Avalanche has a way about him. Even though we both know what we are about to do is illegal, after his words, I'm good with it. That girl doesn't deserve what

I'm assuming she's going through. If it's anything like Frankie and I went through then the sooner we get to her, the better. Nothing will erase her situation, but if it doesn't go on for hours or days that's a good thing in my mind.

No one says a word for about ten minutes. Then something dawns on me.

"How do we know where to go?"

Panther looks at me through the rearview mirror.

"Freak from the Intruders was out where the kids were taken down. He flew his drone around and has their location as it stands at the moment. That's why we're moving in so fast, Malcolm. Once they move her, our chances of finding her get slimmer each day. They might even sell her after they've had their fill. And for her, as you know, the sooner the better. Freak has been flying the drone over the top, up as far as it can go, so they don't clue in on what he's doing. We're about fifteen minutes away. Try to relax. Not sure it will help, friend, but these women know what they are doing. I know you worry about Wildcat, as I do my Nizhoni, or as you know her as Shadow. All I ask is do as you're told, even if you don't agree. Time is of essence and Tink, Shadow, Wildcat, Glory, and the rest of those women have enough on their minds, they don't need any of us to give them anything else to deal with. For years they've been saving people. Let them do what they are good at, Malcolm. Be the backup for any medical issues. And maybe also be some support for Wildcat."

His words hit hard. Yeah, I've always taken my oath

seriously and I tried to help anyone who came through the emergency room, but once they either were admitted or discharged, I have no idea what happens to them. Being in this situation, I will see firsthand what happens at the scene. I might be able to change someone's life in a positive way. My thinking is all over. One thing is for sure, Frankie has grown and matured enough to want to help others despite what happened to her. She found her calling. Now I must find mine.

"Hang on, Malcolm, we are going off road, gonna get bumpy. Make sure you put on the bulletproof vest before getting out of the truck."

I give Panther a nod, grabbing the vest that is on the floor. I've seen them before but I've never had a reason to wear one. I maneuver around until I have it on. Something appears in front of me. When I focus, it's a handgun. Fuck.

"Thanks, but no thanks, Avalanche. Not a believer in those, never have been. I save lives, not take them. No judgment, promise, but I just can't."

"Malcolm, not asking. If you plan to get out of the truck you will be armed. What if someone grabs your Frankie? What are you going to do, throw gauze at them? I'm not trying to be funny, brother. Hook the holster to the back of your jeans and remember it's there, just in case. If by chance you need to use it aim for center mass, largest area on the body, as you well know. We're getting close, Panther's going to turn the headlights out. Don't talk unless necessary."

That's when I notice they both have those earbuds in

their ears like Secret Service people wear. Yeah, they have come prepared. In my narrow life I never gave any thought to what happens when people are taken from their homes to be sold as property to sexual predators. Just the little I've been exposed to is, to say the least, not only heartbreaking for the victims but definitely dangerous for those trying to rescue and save them from a life of horror and abuse.

"Malcolm, we're going to park right down by that bunch of trees. Actually, behind them. We are about maybe a third to a quarter mile away. The Devil's Handmaidens are already hiking in as they left their bikes right off the main road, though as hidden as possible. We should see them pass by if we're lucky. Three of the Intruders are down there in case an unexpected guest chooses to take a ride down. I know for sure that Pussy, Saw, and Tomahawk are experienced with this kind of mission. Pussy drives for the Devil's Handmaidens and also helps when they have a huge number saved from circuits. The other two have been with Tank forever, actually think they kind of grew up in the club. Enforcer is with Tink and the women. Promised Taz he'd keep an eye on her sisters, though my woman, Zoey, isn't thrilled with his presence. They have a hate-hate relationship most time. You know, kind of like siblings do."

I can tell Panther is taking his time trying to explain everything to me. Avalanche gets out of the front seat, opens my door, and motions for me to get out. Then he checks my bulletproof vest and makes sure I put the holster on my jeans right. I couldn't resist being a bit of an asshole to him, though I do it with a smile on my face.

"Thanks, Dad, want to check my ass, make sure I wiped good?"

I watch his eyes get larger on his face as I hear Panther muffle his chuckle. Since I don't know the big man that well, I wait to see what he does. When he offers me his knuckles, I know this could be the beginning of a bro relationship. He gives me a shove back into the truck and shuts the door quietly, just as I see out of the corner of my eye something moving against the driver's side of the truck. I go to reach for the gun at my waist at the same time Avalanche opens the door, grabbing me by the collar. That's when that face appears in the window and, thank God, the big man covered my mouth as I let out a screech. Shadow looks my way, grins, and gives me a little wave as Avalanche gives her his middle finger. Fuck, maybe I'm not made for this kind of shit.

I see figure after figure make their way past Panther's truck until the passenger door opens and Frankie is there. Damn, even at a time like this my mind goes to how hot she is. That short haircut is so fucking sassy on her, showing her beautiful eyes off perfectly. Her skin is glowing, even in the night shade. Between Billie's coloring and Enzo's olive skin tone, my Frankie has a golden caramel skin tone. She leans in toward me so I push the huge duffel bag to the floor and move as much as I can toward her.

"How you doing, Malty? These two taking care of you? How's your back?"

Just like Frankie, risking her life but still worried and concerned about me.

"Hey, keep your head in the game. I'm here, if you fall into a medical situation, just let Panther know. I'm set up with this bag of supplies. Go catch up to them, don't want you wandering alone."

That's when I see the look in her eyes change. She reaches for a strap that's across her chest and brings her, holy shit, it's the Louisville Slugger she had when we were together. She used to love to play softball so one Christmas I bought a personalized one for her. And, apparently, she's kept it. She swings it back around. She touches my face then turns and starts to jog to catch up to the bunch of women risking their lives to save another. Only out here in Bumfuck, Montana because in New York no one cares about anyone else but themselves. And it's getting worse. Avalanche climbs back into the front seat and it's radio silence. I grab the duffel and start going through it so I have an idea of what I have. Panther looks over his shoulder at me.

"If this becomes a thing, meaning you sticking around, let me know if you need anything else. Yoggie was a medic in the military so he gave us a list and we put it together. No pressure, Malcolm, just want to make sure you have everything you need. We've had some touch-and-go situations and even though Yoggie has some training, a doctor would be so much better. We almost lost Raven last year from a gunshot to the chest.

She flatlined like… what, Avalanche, three or four times? Didn't know if she'd ever walk again."

I don't say a word, just take it all in. If I thought Frankie being a New York cop was dangerous, her being a part of this motorcycle club sounds ten times worse.

"Malcolm, totally understand but it's not always like this. Sometimes it's just ranching and taking care of town issues, unless a new human trafficking circuit is discovered. Then the Handmaidens will do whatever is necessary to break it up and save as many as possible. Or sometimes it's just getting the IDs so families can have peace of mind and stop looking at every face that walks by them, thinking it might be their loved ones."

Fuck, how did Panther know what I was thinking? Then I remember the Navajo explanation he gave me yesterday, I think. Not wanting to pry but being the curious fuck that I am, and since we're sitting here, figured I'll ask a question or two. I find out that Panther and his group of men live on his ranch about forty-five minutes to an hour away. They have a stud farm and service, along with breaking wild horses. Panther, Avalanche, Dallas, George, Chicago, and Jersey all were in the military. That's how they met. These two men, along with Jersey, were taken as prisoners of war. Avalanche didn't say anything further on that, and I didn't ask. Panther told an abbreviated story of how he got together with Zoey, or as I know her, Shadow. That was an interesting conversation to say the least because, again, I had to ask if he was ever afraid of her. He turned to face me and said there was no one other than the man sitting next to him that he trusted more with his life. It was easy to see how much he adored his woman.

I get tired of asking questions and after a few they ask me, we go back to silence. I lean my head back and close my eyes, trying to imagine what was going on. Again, Panther must have peeked in my head because he turns to me with those dark eyes and calming voice.

"Nothing has happened yet, Malcolm. They are getting into position. One of the Intruders, think it's Midnight, has taken the east side, high up, and on the west is Rebel. Both are excellent sharpshooters so the team going in has backup, no matter what."

Again, we go the silence mode and just when I'm about to fall asleep, I hear it again and again. Gunfire. When I go to get out of the truck both men turn to me, and I let go of the door handle. Fuck, how do they sit here? Especially Panther, knowing his woman is in danger.

"Breathe, Malcolm. Have faith in your woman's abilities. They train very hard for these types of scenarios. If they need help, they aren't afraid to ask for it. We don't go in unless we are called. We make sure no one gets in or out. Don't forget, we still have Freak with the drone watching the situation, so we have eyes on the scene. This is a well thought-out mission, Malcolm."

So with that explanation, I lean back yet again, though I'm on pins and needles with worry for Frankie and the women she calls her sisters.

EIGHTEEN
'WILDCAT'
FRANKIE

Son of a bitch, I swear to whatever is holy that I wish I was made more like Shadow. These motherfuckers are beyond sick. We think we found five of the six missing women in deplorable conditions. We haven't tried to talk to them yet because Tink wants a better vantage point, so everyone is shifting. From what I can see the women are doubled up in the tents, each one with one ratty-ass blanket. Most of them are walking around like zombies so probably drugged up. There are also a few younger women or maybe even girls, can't tell. They are huddled off by one of the huts, peeling potatoes, I think. No sign of Cici yet.

Glancing around, something seems off. There are no guards posted around their camp. And besides the women, we've seen no one else. There is smoke coming out of the big cabin's chimney though. In my earpiece I hear Tink telling everyone to hold. I see Glory trying to make her way down to scope it out. Before she takes a few steps, I quietly whisper, "Check for trip wires." I see heads start to shift back and forth then I hear the words like *shit, damn,* and *fuck*. Tink calls Glory back before she gets too far into whatever they set up. Motherfuckers probably did it to keep the women in. I'm thinking the one we don't see tried to get out, poor girl.

Suddenly there's a scream like nothing I've heard before in my life. It was full of pain and suffering coming from the big cabin. All the other women shift toward each other, two putting their hands over their ears. The younger girls move slowly toward the women. They are brought in close, all in the middle of the circle, so when you first glance that way you don't see the girls. We hear voices but can't make out what is being said.

This is the part of our rescues that sucks big time. We can't just run in and sometimes waiting is the hardest thing to do when someone is being brutally tortured or raped. Just about all the Devil's Handmaidens sisters have experienced some form of brutality in their lives, so we do understand. Bottom line is to get out as many as we can alive. With that thought, I lean back on my calves, taking a minute or two to breathe and try to relax. The screams have lessened but the agony hasn't. When the door opens, I almost vomit seeing a very heavyset man naked as the day he was born with a huge cigar hanging from his mouth.

"One of you bitches get in here now. She's fuckin' passed out again, and worth shit if she's not awake and fighting. Come on, don't make me pick someone. Let's go, whores, move it. Where are those girlies we like to play with? Never mind, Freckles, get your ass in here now."

I watch in horror as a woman with brownish hair moves from the circle. Two of the women try to hold her back but she shrugs them off. I can see she's got bruises all over her body, as she's barely got any clothing on. She walks toward the cabin and when within reach, he pulls the cigar out of his mouth and grinds his mouth on hers. She doesn't moan, cry, or scream, just lets him do what he wants. When he pushes her to her knees, I have to close my eyes. I can't watch. That's when my earbud whispers to me, "We're going. Try and be observant, stay close to each other. No noise 'til we pass the perimeter. If seen then shoot, otherwise, let's get as close as we can before we turn this into a massacre. Freak says, as far as he can see with the drone, there doesn't seem to be any traps going directly in. On the backside he made out a few dug-up spots, he's thinking they are mines or something. He also spotted a freshly dug grave, so not sure how many or who. Keep your eyes open and watch each other's backs. We move in five, four, three, two, one. GO."

Next to me is Peanut on one side and Dottie on the other. Slowly and methodically, we move toward the small area, trying to watch every step we take. Every single one of us has a black knit hat on our heads to hide our hair and the color. We have nighttime riding glasses on because it helps with glare and manages the clarity of what's in front of us. We do have night vision goggles, but sometimes they hamper our vision. Looking past

Dottie, I see Yoggie and off to his other side I see Enforcer.

When we finally make it through to what I guess you could call an overgrown campsite, we break into teams of four or five. Our team is Yoggie, Enforcer, Dottie, Peanut, and me. As we start to move toward the quarters, I see all the other teams branching out so we are coming in from all directions. The circle of women must have felt our presence because one by one they turn and look our way. Like a synchronized dance, we all raise our fingers to our lips and motion for them to be quiet and to stay where they are, not to move at all. Surprisingly, they all listen except one of the young girls. She makes a move to run to us and one of the women gently grabs her, pulling the girl into her, hugging her tightly, and whispering in her ear. As I watch, the girl starts to cry silently and that woman absorbs every ounce of pain coming from that girl, wrapping her arms around her even tighter. I look over to Dottie and she reads my look, nodding. No matter what, they are all getting out of this shithole tonight.

Suddenly, out of nowhere, we hear a four-wheeler making its way to where we are. Before even thinking about it, we all move quickly to take cover. Dottie, Peanut, and I crawl into one of the huts and, fuck, what a goddamn mistake. These aren't to give those folks somewhere out of the weather. This is where those men abuse these women. The smell literally covers you when you crawl in, and I guess you can call it a sleeping bag is covered in all kinds of shit. Peanut scrunches it up and throws it in the corner. We can almost stand but stay on our knees, keeping silent. The flap swings open, and we all reach for our guns when we see a small head poke in before crawling inside. The young girl is short enough to stand and she does this off to the side as the woman who grabbed her follows. No one says a word but something comes to mind, so I reach into my kutte and pull out my deputy star. I see the sparkle in the girl's eyes as the woman is more guarded. That kind of tells me she's not trusting of police, so somewhere she's experienced abuse from someone who should have protected her.

They both slowly move toward us until Peanut waves them to stop. The girl leans a bit closer. The smell from her is so bad but not one of us turns away. We would never make her feel bad so as Shadow would tell us, suck it up. We all carry Vicks nasal inhalers so I reach back into my kutte, feel for it, and turn so she won't see me. I quickly take a breath then put it away before turning back to them. As we wait, I take in their appearance, which if graded from one to ten; one being the worst and ten being the best. I'd say they are maybe a four or five. Crust in their eyes, skin blotchy, very thin and malnourished from the color of their bodies underneath all the bruises and goddamn bite marks. The young girl seems to be in better shape than the woman. Either she's new here or they are going to sell her off for large amounts of money and she must be kept in good shape, while the woman can be abused constantly because when they're done she'll be buried next to whoever is in the grave in the back.

Suddenly, we hear gunfire so I reach for the girl and Dottie grabs the woman. We all drop to the ground, though the three of us pull out our guns. I get to my knees off to the side of the entrance as everyone stays close to the walls, so if someone tries to come in, they have to turn their heads to see who's in here. Before I can think about it, I reach behind me and grab my Sig Sauer. I look to the woman who is watching us like a hawk. When I move toward her, she puts the girl behind her. Yeah, mothering type, for sure. In a very hushed voice, I do what is necessary.

"We are here to get all of you out. Is there a girl here who is called Cici? I'm going to give this to you for protection; we have to move out. Stay in here, spread out that bag, and make it look like someone might be sleeping in it. Timing is everything. I've taken the safety off so if you feel threatened by someone, just aim for their chest and fire. Shoot to kill."

I give her the gun and an extra magazine. She drops her head for a quick second then looks at me, a huge smile on her face. She's been here a bit; I can tell by her teeth. That's okay, we'll get them fixed up when they get to the ranch. The shooting starts again sporadically. Dottie taps my shoulder then points to the flap. I nod and one by one we leave, not saying another word. Detachment is the hardest part of doing this. I hate leaving victims to fend for themselves, but we have to look at the whole picture.

Peanut starts toward the largest cabin with Dottie and me following closely. She raises a hand and stops. I start to look around as I feel eyes on us but not sure if it's a threat or hope. When I see three women peering out from a tent, I give them a nod and motion for them to go back in. They stare for a second or two then follow my orders. Just as we start to move again, I see Tink, Shadow, and Duchess. Shadow lifts her hand, telling us to go around the back. When we get back there the smell is horrific, as it seems these idiots have been pissing and shitting behind the cabin. *Lucky fucking us*, I think to myself. I take my bandanna from my neck and cover my mouth with it. Learned a long time ago to keep one on me. And it smells just like fresh laundry.

Once in position, I hit my earbud twice to let Tink and Shadow know we are in position. Right before the explosion, it is so quiet I am freaking out. Then the large boom and all hell breaks loose. We hold as Tink, Shadow, and Duchess breach the front of the cabin. I hear gunfire and know it's coming from us, then nothing.

"Wildcat, get your ass in here now. Be careful! We got one hiding in the spare bedroom door, barricaded in, but we'll get him. Need help, oh my God, what did they do to you, sweetie? No, don't move. Stay there. Shadow, put pressure on that. Wildcat, get in here and have one of them call in Malcolm. We're going to lose Cici if we don't move fast."

I'm already on the move when I hear Dottie quietly telling someone to get Malcolm here stat. I check the door first then slowly open it. The cabin is not too shabby but you can tell it's been used. At first, I don't see anything, but under the stairs is a weird bed with, fuck, a goddamn cage underneath it. Two dog bowls are in the cage zip-tied to the sides of the walls, guess so they won't spill. Water is filthy and the food has maggots in it. I can feel my head starting to pound, but I keep looking and that's when I see them. My eyes take in the scene but my mind can't process it at first. When it does, I literally run toward the body that is in something like those medieval contraptions where they have someone's head and hands in the stocks. This had to be similar to a pillory that was used primarily for public humiliation, though instead of her head and hands stuck in the holes this has a long piece of wood that she's lying on, with her arms stretched above her stuck in boards that are held together by a lock. Same with her legs, she's spread-eagled on this thing, which gives these motherfuckers access to her twenty-four seven. When I get to her, I kneel down and touch her forehead gently. She doesn't move and she's barely breathing. If she's lucky, she was unconscious through most of their abuse. I grab the bottle of water Heartbreaker hands me and I pour just a little on her mouth. At first nothing, but human instinct kicks in. She struggles to open her eyes but when she does, she swallows the little bit of liquid. She turns her head and I'm looking into the most devastated brown eyes that I know deep to my soul I'll never forget.

"Please kill me. Don't save me, just put a bullet in my head. I don't want to live."

By this time the cabin is filling up. Some of my

Handmaiden sisters are standing close, but I don't care. Need to get her head on straight.

"Are you Cici? Just nod for me if you are. Good, nice to meet you, Cici, I'm Wildcat. We're here to take you back to your parents. No, listen to me, honey. No one knows what you just went through, but please stay with me for a few minutes. They grabbed you yesterday and we are here now to take you back. What about the other women? How long have they been held against their will? I'm not trying to upset you but, Cici, this only works if you want to live. Fight, sweetie, with everything in you, and just maybe this will take a turn and you'll survive. I didn't say you'll be okay because I'm not going to lie to you, nothing is ever going to be 'okay.'"

"You think? How do you know that? I don't want my parents to know what they did to me. Wildcat, I don't feel too good."

Looking at her color, she seems a bit grayish-white. When I take a closer look its then I see the puddle of blood underneath her. Son of a bitches.

"Cici, hey, honey, listen to me. A few years ago, something similar happened to me. Yeah, I'm telling the truth and believe me, I wanted to die. And sometimes I still do but then they win, and I won't let them win. Cici, did they sodomize you? This is very important, please tell me. Promise, I won't say a word to your parents. Hey, Peanut, get Malcolm in here right now."

She must recognize the urgency in my voice because she runs out screaming for Malcolm. That's when it hits me, where the hell are all the assholes responsible for this human destruction? Then I hear the first wail and it brings joy to my heart. That tells me Shadow is at work and we will be listening to her special kind of music for some time. I lean down and look Cici right in the eyes.

"You hear that? They will pay and continue to pay until Shadow's done. Then she will put them to ground. None of them will walk away from this or live to tell their sick stories. That I can promise you, beautiful girl."

The tears roll down her cheeks. I move the blanket Peanut covered her with to check how badly she's bleeding. I see Enforcer making his way over with Yoggie.

"Need something to cut through that cuff and lock. It's not a standard cuff so whatever you can and as fast as you can. She's lost a lot of blood, and from the disaster on her arm they were shooting her up with something. Dehydrated, beaten, raped, and sodomized in less than twenty-four hours. I hope to Christ Shadow takes twice as long with them."

Yoggie reaches into a bag and pulls out a huge keychain with keys on it. I have no idea but watch as he patiently goes through each key. When he puts in a key that opens the cuff, I hear a soft whimper but nothing else. I feel Cici's wrist for a pulse and it's there but faint and thready.

I feel his presence before I see him. Malcolm is moving quickly to me, Avalanche following with the huge duffel bag. When he's close, Malcolm reaches for me, squeezing tightly for just a second. Then he turns his attention to the person on the floor covered in a blanket only. Cici's arms are now free and Peanut is rubbing them to get circulation flowing back through. When Yoggie gets to where her legs are cuffed, he looks once then twice before his eyes find mine.

"These on her ankles are police-issued handcuffs. Need to talk to Sheriff George, maybe one of the Thunder Cloud Knuckle Brotherhood followers is on a police force somewhere. Not here in Timber-Ghost, but close by. Come on, Malcolm, look at her, she needs medical attention now."

I move so Malcolm can assess Cici's condition but can't see his face. When his body tenses up, I know he's getting the full picture now.

"Hurry up, Yoggie, need to check out her injuries. Especially the one bleeding so heavily. I'm going to try and start an IV to get some fluids into her. Quickest way to rehydrate her."

As we all work to keep Cici alive, it dawns on me that today we won. We not only rescued Cici, but all these other women and young girls are coming back to the ranch with us. And in time they will realize they are given the best gift of all: a second chance.

Another wail, louder this time, hangs in the air as they come more frequently. I can't help the smile that covers my face, knowing they will all get what they deserve. When I glance down, Cici is looking at me, eyes still filled with tears but she has a tiny smile on her face. Then I look to Malcolm, who is trying to keep his feelings from Cici, but I've known the man my entire life. It's killing him to see the damage done to her. Though when he lifts his head and takes in both Cici and me smiling as we hear another pain-filled shout, he then smiles right along with us. Yeah, today is a great day as the good folks won this fight, though the war is still raging.

NINETEEN
'MALCOLM'
MALTY

The damage that was done to Cici in such a short period of time shocks me. How can a human being do that kind of cruelty to someone and not have any repercussions? When Yoggie finally got the cuffs off Cici and we tried to pull her off that piece of torture wood, she let out such a high-pitched screech it hurt my ears. I know I'll never forget the agony behind it. So with the help of Yoggie, Panther, Avalanche, and Enforcer we slowly flipped her to the side, and my God, her entire back had been whipped and torn to shreds. Not only was she in pain because of the injuries, but she was placed on the board while bleeding so the blood dried. Fuck. I look around and am shocked when Tink stops in front of me with two, no, three bottles of water.

"Try this, Malcolm, it might help. I would give her something for pain because, no matter what, that is going to hurt bad. It's going to reopen some of those marks and pull off some of the loose skin. Wildcat, talk to her, get her out of her head. Maybe talking with you will distract her some. Yeah, I know, but best we can do. Enforcer, put a call out to Tank and tell him we are going to need the copter to get her out of here. There's a clear field about three minutes to the north of us. Right now, as you can hear, Shadow is playing. Duchess and Glory are checking out the other women. We've found a couple of shallow graves, so may be able to match DNA and give some families closure. Okay, I'll be back. Get her ready for transport, no matter what you must do. I have a feeling that all of the degenerates aren't here so we don't want to get caught here with all these innocents around. Especially in the shape they all are in."

I watch that tiny woman walk away, thinking that looks can be deceiving. I'd hate to have to go against her ever. Something waves in front of my face so I focus and see Yoggie has a syringe loaded already.

"Cici. Cici, hey, look at me. I want to make you as comfortable as possible. Do you have any allergies?"

She opens her mouth but nothing comes out. Frankie pours a tiny amount of water on her lips as Cici shakes her head. When she can, she again shocks the hell out of me.

"I can't take pain medication. I hurt my knee in high school and got hooked on opioids. Took me almost nine months to come clean. Don't want to go down that road again."

As Cici is talking, the red-haired club sister of Frankie's walks up close. She must have heard what Cici said because she takes a knee next to my girl.

"Cici, right? I was also hooked on opioids, so I get why you're worried. Listen though, what they are about to do is going to be excruciatingly painful. Malcolm isn't going to give you a lot of pain medication, just enough to not only calm you down but take the edge off. If you want, I'll be right here with Wildcat. You can squeeze my hand as hard as you want, even break a finger or two if that will get you through this."

I see Cici look to the hand held out to her and I realize Heartbreaker's fingers look to have already been broken. Cici asks the question.

"Yeah, my fingers have been broken already because I chose drugs instead of a person in trouble. You aren't doing that, Cici. This is called surviving. So can the guys do their thing and get you ready for transport? Honey, you need medical attention and not only for your back. You're losing blood fast and you know what I'm trying to say in mixed company. Please let them get you from this contraption so we can move you to where the helicopter will land."

"Will you be able to come with me in the helicopter? Heartbreaker, that's what you said your name is, right? I don't want to be alone, especially with a bunch of men."

My stomach flips because this isn't just physical but also emotional and psychological abuse. Those fuckers altered this poor girl's life forever. How the hell do these women and men do this all the time? It feels like my heart and soul are being pulled from my body. I feel a small hand on my lower back and turn to see Frankie's eyes on mine. She mouths, "You okay?" Yeah, that's just like her, always worrying about everyone. I nod just as Cici tells Heartbreaker she's ready to get out of here. Thank Christ.

Yoggie grabs two bottles and another syringe. When he shows me the medication, I nod. Good choice giving her more of a relaxer like Xanax. The second is Tramadol. I'm going to use the middle dosage of sixty mg/ml. This should not only help with the pain but these two drugs will hopefully put Cici into a form of twilight, which will allow us to move her.

I lift the filthy blanket off Cici, checking her hip for somewhere to give the shot. She's a mess, so I give Yoggie a look then point with the syringe to her arm. He nods and after a quick swipe of an alcohol pad, which seems stupid but it's my training, I inject the medication into Cici's arm. Within, shit, like four minutes or so her eyes get heavy. Both Frankie and Heartbreaker are softly talking to her. With the help of the men, we again lean Cici and the wooden contraption to the side and start pouring the water on her to loosen the dried blood. The more water we use, the horror of what she went through is becoming very apparent. After the third bottle, when we go to put her down, Tink comes running in with two more bottles of water. She hands them off and immediately leaves.

Now that all the water has been poured over Cici's back, we gently put her back on the ground. I give the women a look so they know we are about to literally pull her off the wood. Yoggie moves to her feet and places his foot on the board she's been cuffed to. Frankie does the same and I see their eyes meet. They'll make great partners because they already have a relationship and seem to read each other. Back to the matter at hand. Panther is on one side and Avalanche is on my side.

"Doc, move outta the way. No way we're putting ya at risk. We'll lift her, you make sure she comes off that board, no matter what. Be prepared, Malcolm, no matter how many drugs you shoot into her, she is going to make sounds you've never heard in your life before. This is going to be torture for her, so let's do this quickly. How do you want her once she's off, on her stomach, maybe? So you can get a good look of the damage done."

I just nod while moving out of the way. I'm between Avalanche and Frankie and all of them are looking at me for direction. Shit, okay, we can do this.

"Okay, on three, pull her off. So one, two, three…."

The sounds coming from Cici aren't even human. They sound like a wild animal being tortured or killed. At the same moment we start to pull her off, we hear another scream coming from whatever Shadow is doing. Panther glances toward the door but never stops pulling Cici up. We hear weird noises coming as her body is pulled from the board. When she is free her head hangs a bit, though Heartbreaker is holding on tightly. Once the guys turn her so I can see her back, I feel the bile come up my throat but I swallow it down.

It looks like raw meat. Besides being whipped, she was also burned with either cigarettes or cigars. On her one shoulder I can even see the striations of muscle through the deep open cut. Immediately, I move the duffel bag closer as I pull out saline and gauze. Yoggie is right across from me and together we clean Cici's back as best we can. With sterile scissors he cuts off layers of hanging skin that already are turning black. Using butterfly strips to try to close the worst ones, we work our way down her back. Yoggie reaches over, pushing on my shoulder, then looks down. Goddamn it.

Looks like Cici has some form of a rupture or prolapsed anus due to severe sexual assault. She'll need surgery to repair that. Son of a bitch. Yoggie is monitoring her stats while both Panther and Avalanche help me with her many injuries. Once we have her as stable as possible, I look around for something to put her on. Yoggie dives into the bottom of the duffle bag and pulls out another nylon bag. Then he pulls out something that looks like a mix between a yoga mat and a banner. He flips it open, grabs some poles to support it, then lays it right next to Cici. Well, what the hell, I have never seen anything like that before.

"Malcolm, we used these a lot when I was in the military. Easy enough to pack in your gear and helps when someone needs to be moved carefully. I'd say try and put her on her side. Or as best we can. Gotta get a move on, chopper is on its way."

Together as a team we prop Cici on the makeshift stretcher and between Yoggie, Panther, Avalanche, and Enforcer, they pick her up. I know they are trying to protect me, but damn, I feel useless. Well, until Panther tells me to lead the way. With Heartbreaker and Frankie on either side of me, we carefully walk toward the field. It looks to have been cleared out recently so maybe that was their plan to get rid of or sell these women.

In the distance I hear something, not sure what. Looking up, that's when I see the drone circling the area.

"Yeah, that's our brother, Freak, keeping eyes in the sky. This way we are covered and no surprises, Malcolm. Ain't our first rodeo, Doc."

I look behind me to see all the men smirking or grinning. Yeah, gotta find something to smile about when dealing with this kind of stuff. We set Cici down and we all surround her. Heartbreaker is down on a knee, holding her hand, talking to her even though she's unconscious. That's when I hear the swooshing sound. I tilt my head and when it comes into view my mouth drops open. *How in the fuck does Tink's dad have one of them?* I think to myself.

"Malcolm, we all asked the same question first time we saw that thing. It's an Airbus EC145 and from what Zoey has told me, it's not Tank's. He has a friend who, let's just say acquired this machine. He leaves it out here in a hanger for Tank to use when he needs it."

I watch as the big bird lands and immediately Cici is lifted and brought to the side door. She's loaded up, then Heartbreaker gets in beside her. Everyone looks to me. Oh, holy mother of God, they want me to go too.

"Malcolm, need a doctor or medic to go with. Once we clean up the trash, we'll meet you at the hospital."

I look into Frankie's eyes and realize there isn't anything I wouldn't do for her, so I nod and carefully get in the copter. The pilot points to the seat directly behind him. Once everyone is settled, he gives a hand signal twirling his finger in the air. Before I can even take a breath, he lifts up in the air and off we go.

One thing pops into my head. I'd hate to be any of those men down there because we're lucky enough to fly away. All they have to look forward to is knowing today is the day, after Shadow plays with them, they will take their last breath and die. What a sobering thought.

TWENTY
'SHADOW'
ZOEY

My body is itchy from all the dried blood and guts on it. Not to mention it's humid as fuck out here. Not my choice to work someone over in the goddamn forest, but I'm pretty flexible. Out of the nine men we caught, six are dead. Some in multiple pieces, had to get creative this time. Needed them to talk quickly and shut up their screams of pain, though it's like music to my ears.

Looking at the last three, one is fading fast. I move toward him as he's hanging upside down from a tree. Blood is pooling under him, dripping from his nose and ears. Probably from the blunt force trauma. I'm pretty sure between Rebel and me together, we fractured his skull. Oh well, shit happens as they say. A small part of me feels bad, he's a younger guy but, fuck, he made the wrong decisions. Plus, he was one of the assholes in that cabin with Cici. He was actually pushing his junk into his jeans when we busted in. That's when he shit his pants. Yeah, pretty nasty but it got worse, especially after I saw what they did to Cici. Now he's going to die scared, alone, and hopefully realizing the mistakes he's made in his short life. I mean, this is when I get emotional, if I can even call it that. He's someone's kid, brother, cousin. Seriously doubt he's got a wife, don't seem to respect women much.

When we stripped him, his dick still had Cici's blood on it, so that tells me more than I ever wanted to know. Well, he is now covered in his own blood. I look to Dani and nod. She reaches for her knife and cuts the rope. He falls hard to the ground but not a sound comes from his mouth. Somehow, he manages to roll over and moan. When he does open his eyes, they are blown. The whites of his eyes are pinkish and his pupils are blown. I could just let him suffer and die, but I'm not that person anymore. So, I approach him. When I'm beside him, I crouch down and lift his head.

"Anything else you want to tell me, kid?"

He starts to shake and I think it finally penetrated that this is it.

"I don't want to die. Why do you have to kill me? If you let me go, I'll work with you. I can change, give me a chance. Fuck, lady, I'm only twenty-one years old."

"Yeah, you dick, and the girl you raped with your buddies was twenty years old. She did nothing but want to live her life. Wrong place, wrong time."

"What the hell are you talking about? Oh, wow, you haven't figured it out yet. This was planned. Check out the players. That girl was bought and paid for with a huge bag of money. We were just the beginning for her.

She was sold to a dude overseas. Guess you're going to have to figure out who did this to her. You can kill me, but there will be five or ten more to take my place."

My mind is spinning. Who the fuck would want to sell Cici? I doubt her folks, so maybe the boyfriend? Wow, damn, we know nothing about the victim. We took everything at face value because Tank knew her parents. What the hell did we get involved with?

Hearing the rattling people have before they pass, I look down. I don't have to do a thing; his time is coming to an end.

"Anyone you want me to tell, kid?"

"No, both of my folks are in jail and my brother couldn't care less. And my name isn't kid, it's Noah."

"Well, Noah, I wish to Christ we had met under way different circumstances. I'm Shadow."

"I don't have the right to ask, but will you stay with me?"

Instead of answering, I lean back and sit on my ass. I reach out and grab Noah's hand and give it a squeeze. He tries to squeeze back but doesn't have the strength. I hear his chanting before I see him. Panther sits right next to me continuing to chant. This is his way to send Noah off to a better place. That's why my ol' man is a better person than I'll ever be. He always gives people second and third chances. I'm a one and done kind of woman. Noah looks between the two of us, then closes his eyes for a brief second.

"Never thought the last thing I'd see is an Indian chanting with a woman with a skull tattoo. Life is full of surprises. Gotta thank you, Shadow, for doing this, more than my own family's ever done for me. I'll tell you to check out Cici's close friends. Especially look at the female friends with her boyfriend, Kevin."

My head jerks up. How did he know the boyfriend's name? As my mind is spinning Panther stops chanting for a minute. Then he leans down toward Noah.

"Noah, tell Zoey how you know that man's name? Make that be your last good deed you do in this life."

Noah looks at me as the crackles in his chest get louder. Won't be long now. His eyes close then pop right back open. He finds the strength to squeeze my hand.

"I know this because that dude Kevin is my cousin. Some chick had it out for Cici because they were dating. She wanted Kevin for her own, like he's a prize or something. Her daddy is rich, owns some manufacturing company in Billings. That's what I know..."

Noah starts to cough as Panther starts to chant. Within a minute or two this young guy is dead. For what... money, power, dominance? Who the fuck knows. I go to wipe my face and feel the wet on my cheeks. Oh God no, can't show weakness, not in front of my sisters. Rebel looks down, her eyes are wet too. Yeah, what badasses are we, crying over some little weasel who made the wrong choices in his short life. I watch as Rebel turns and walks away, while I feel Panther's arms pull me close. Damn, this job just keeps getting harder and harder. I reach over and close Noah's eyes. What a fuckin' waste.

* * *

I can taste the iron in my mouth from blood spatter. The last motherfucker just took his last breath. Squirt, Dani, and Kitty are burying the bodies, or what's left of them. Got some good info though. Rebel was a huge help to me today. She never once turned her head, lost purpose, or got physically sick. Some of the shit she did was new stuff to me. As sick as it is, I'm glad she's working side by side with me. Up by the cabins my dad, Sheriff George, has some deputies going over everything. All the women were transferred to the hospital. My club sisters have been waiting around for me to finish. I tried to tell Goldilocks to go back to the ranch but she refused, saying we work our missions together from start to end. So now it's the middle of the night and we're all getting bit up by mosquitos while Rebel, Squirt, Dani, and Kitty are covered in all kinds of body muck and blood. Kiwi and Dottie also had some shit on them when Rebel and I took a break earlier. Personally, I had to pee and refused to piss down my legs. So found a quiet spot in the woods, peed, drank some water, ate a protein peanut butter bar, and tried to make sense of what I've been told. This isn't the Thunder Cloud Knuckle Brotherhood calling the shots. Well, sort of, but this is just the hatred that is moving through our country. I'm no fuckin' saint by any means, but what I do is for the purpose of trying to stop human trafficking and the abuse of innocent people. There isn't a day that goes by I'm not thankful for finding Goldilocks and forming the Devil's

Handmaidens Motorcycle Club with her. We have the best of the best because each of us have experienced hell on earth. This kind of evil scares the shit out of me because there is no endgame in sight. They do it because they can. Add money to it and they feel untouchable. I start to pick up my shit, which I'll have to clean when we get back to the ranch or clubhouse, whichever.

Hearing a branch snap, I turn, hand on my gun. Rebel smirks at me.

"What, gonna shoot me, Shadow? Then who's going to help you with this kind of shit? Not many of our sisters have the stomach for this. You need me, sister, don't forget it and, yeah, I know how hard that is for you. So what do you think, is that boyfriend Kevin involved or just a sorry sap? Gotta have Raven do a deep dive, see if he was fucking around on Cici. That I could see, some stupid young woman falling for him and then he decides he wants to stay with Cici. Here, let me help you with that shit."

Together we keep walking around with our phone flashlights on. Well, until a bright light starts toward us. Of course it's got to be Big Bird, my pain in my ass. He's singing the dwarf song from *Cinderella*.

"Hi ho, hi ho, we're off to work we go. Zoey's made a mess hi ho, hi ho, and we have to clean it up again. Hi ho, hi ho."

Behind him is a line of his team, Devil's Handmaidens, and Intruders all singing off-key and using the wrong words. I know the thought behind it and that warms my heart. That big mountain of a man has a unique way of knowing how this shit has been bothering me. Avalanche walks directly toward me, pulling close just as the wet in my eyes rolls down my face. I hear the group of folks walking around, picking up tools and shit as Big Bird holds me close, never saying a thing.

Not sure but maybe I need to have a conversation with Goldilocks. I don't want to quit doing this, but maybe we can switch it up a bit. I don't mind the blood and guts, it's the emotional side like this kid Noah. He didn't have a chance in life and made really bad decisions that led him to my path. Also, I know Spirit at the sanctuary wouldn't mind helping in certain situations. As my ol' man always is telling me, life is always evolving and we need to keep up with it. Maybe my life is finally moving in the right direction and that's why everything is getting under my skin, who the fuck knows.

"Listen to him, skull anii', he's right. We make our own paths in this life. You need to be a part of this work because it allows you to remove the demons in your soul. No, listen to me, I'm not joking around right now. Find a way to walk both paths of your life. My brother and I have had to do the exact same thing. Don't ever think you are alone because you have Panther and me, along with our team, always behind you. Now if you're okay, I'm gonna let you go and say something to piss you off. Give me your best, Zoey. I always will have your back, lil' sister."

My God, he's trying to kill me. We've always had a

kind of love-hate relationship. We both love Panther and at times like each other, while other times can't stand the sight of the other. He just opened his heart to me, showing me how much he truly cares. He's my brother of choice. I feel a peace wash over me right before he pushes me away.

"Damn, woman, you got me all wet. Hey now, don't go there. Why the fuck is the enforcer of the Devil's Handmaidens leaving tears on my T-shirt? Are you getting soft? Damn. gonna need to talk to both Panther and Tink, maybe you can become the sister who keeps the ranch clean and milks the cows."

I hear the snickers and chuckles but never move my eyes from his. When they start to sparkle, I give him a small smile. Then I let loose.

"You dumbass, Big Bird, I have severe allergies and have been in the woods for hours. I'm not crying, it's a reaction to all the trees, pollen, and mold. Now before you put your big foot in your mouth, let's get this cleaned up. I need a shower, like yesterday. Rebel, come on, sister, let these peons finish this shit up. We've done our job."

Without another word, I turn and stomp my way toward where the larger camp is located. Rebel catches up with me and gives me a shoulder bump.

"As big of an asshole as he can be, gotta love that big man."

I look at my sister and smile. Hugely.

"Yeah, guess you're right, Rebel. We need to find that man an ol' lady. Hey, what about you?"

Rebel's cheeks turn pink but she shakes her head.

"Nope, we aren't each other's type. But I agree, he's a good catch."

Now I'm really interested as to why my club sister knows that her and Big Bird don't mesh. This should be interesting.

TWENTY-ONE
'WILDCAT'
FRANKIE

I'm sitting in the waiting room with Heartbreaker as we wait for Cici to get out of surgery. Her folks are on the way but she began to hemorrhage in the helicopter, so once here they took her right in. I don't even know where she was bleeding from, but I think it was her back end. I heard Malcolm talking to Yoggie about something that was done to her that made something rupture. Not sure but thought that's what he said.

Malcolm and Yoggie are getting cleaned up. One of the emergency room nurses gave them both some scrubs and told them to use the employee locker room to clean up. Not sure how Malty is holding up, but he did a phenomenal job under such stress. I hope he gets why we do what we do as a club. I know that both Panther and Avalanche talked with him. Bottom line though is, it's his decision what happens now. I do know my feelings haven't changed, even over the last couple of years I've been out here. I want the very best for him as he deserves it. If we can agree to try again, I'm on board. If Malcolm decides he just wants to be friends, I'm cool with that, though it's not what I want. *We'll see*, I think to myself.

I hear footsteps then see both William and Sherrie coming toward us with my parents following behind.

"Frankie, my God, how is she? Can we see her, please? What happened?"

Before I can say a word, I see the guys making their way to us.

"Can you hang on for a second, Sherrie? I believe Yoggie and Malcolm can explain better with what's happened to Cici. I can tell you she's in surgery and from what the last nurse told us, it could be a couple of hours. Here are the guys now."

Malcolm and Yoggie, both in scrubs, stop within our group. Mom and Dad are on either side of me so the guys squeeze in. I tell both that Sherrie and William just got here and need an update. Yoggie looks to Malcolm, who then looks to me. I can read what he's asking. How much do I want him to share?

"The truth, Malty. They deserve the truth."

With that he turns and gives a brief overview of Cici's injuries and what they were trying to fix with the surgery. I watch as Sherrie leans into William, whose face is gray. I can see the shaking of his hands as he pulls his wife closer, holding her tightly. When Malcolm finishes, William quietly thanks him. Then he tells us they are going to take a seat in the waiting area. Once they are gone, Yoggie gives Malcolm a man crack on the shoulders and leans in giving me a side hug.

"Gotta get movin'. My Bae and your club are still up at that cabin so need to go pick up Olivia since Angel is working. If you need anything, just reach out. I'll fill in the sheriff tomorrow. We need to get together, Wildcat, figure out a schedule for you. Maybe have Tink and Bae there so we can coordinate shit. Give me a text once she's outta surgery. Kid's got a long road ahead of her. Just a suggestion between us, Wildcat. Try and get her to stay at the ranch. Sometimes too much love can be smothering. Just sayin'. Later."

We watch Yoggie walk away before Malcolm turns to me and asks the question I knew he would.

"Who the hell is Bae and what does that mean, Frankie?"

I smile and grab his hand.

"Bae means 'before anyone else' and that's what Yoggie calls Glory. Shit, did you know that he's with Glory? Probably not, we've had no time for you to meet all of my sisters. From the little I caught during Glory's drama; they were hooking up. Yoggie wanted more but Glory was afraid because she's older than him. As you can see, it worked out for them. Now, let's go grab some seats. Don't know about you, but I'm totally exhausted. I'm sure sooner or later Sheriff George is going to want a statement. Good thing is we saved all those women and young girls. Tomorrow, intake will start. That's a long couple of days, but we need to make sure the ranch is the right place for those victims to stay. Sometimes they need more in-depth care. We have connections now throughout the United States. Maybe you could find time to be on hand to help Dr. Cora with the medical part of everything. I don't know what she does during intake, but I know it's very thorough."

We head into the waiting area where Cici's parents are talking, while my parents are sitting a little bit away, probably to give them some space. I make my way to my mom, who stands and hugs me tightly.

"I'm so very proud of you, Frankie. What you and your club are doing is so needed. I know it's dangerous but from what I've seen, each of you have a job. Thank you to all of you for what you do. I think coming out here is good for you, daughter of my heart. You seem centered and happy. For that I'm thrilled, though it crushes that little hope of you coming back home to New York."

As Mom and I talk, I see my dad and Malcolm going back and forth over what, I don't know. In some ways it's like none of that horrific shit happened. Malcolm has always blended right in with my family. I mean, for Christ's sake, my sister and nephews are at his place watching his fur babies. The more I take time to think about what happened to Malcolm and me, I have to believe we were both worked by Michael. Oh, that's another problem we need to talk about. I already know that Shadow isn't letting him walk away. We had this urgent situation with Cici, but he can't stay on ice forever.

I don't know how long we sat here. Dad and

Malcolm eventually fell asleep. Well, until some of my sisters showed up with food and beverages. Didn't realize how hungry I was until I unwrapped one of Momma Diane's combo sandwiches. William and Sherrie joined us but you could see the strain on their faces. It had to be after midnight by the time the doctor came out looking for Cici's family.

The whole bunch of us stepped back to let William and Sherrie speak to the doctor. As she passed, Sherrie reached out and grabbed my hand. I took that as it was okay that we supported them, so we did by surrounding them in front of the doctor.

"Are you Cici's parents? And these people are?"

Sherrie looks around then back at the doctor.

"These are Cici's family too. They were the ones who searched while risking their lives to find her and bring her here in a helicopter. Doctor, how is our daughter?"

He looks around first, taking in our kuttes, before he wipes his forehead and looks back at Cici's parents.

"We were able to repair the lower intestines. Well, we had to remove some of it then did the repair. The rupture we also fixed. Unfortunately, there was so much damage we had to remove one of her fallopian tubes. She seems to be resting comfortably in the recovery room. She will be moved to the intensive care unit for at least the next twelve to twenty-four hours. If she continues to show progress, then she will be placed in the step-down unit. Plan on her being here between three to five days. Once she's settled, I'll have one of the nurses show you where she's at."

I hear William thanking the doctor as I turn around. Before I can take a few steps, someone grabs my arm so I turn to face them. It's the doctor, so I pull on Malcolm's arm to stop him too. The doctor looks down at me then at Malcolm.

"You're part of that women's motorcycle club on the outskirts of town? Sorry. I'm asking because we've been told that your president, I believe she goes by Tink, is funding the new area here for children's diseases. Could you tell her, I mean your president, that I'm grateful. My daughter is a Type 1 diabetic, so having that wing here will save my wife hours of driving to Billings or Bozeman to see the specialist. You all do such good things for our town. It's so appreciated. Thanks."

When he stretches out his hand, I grab it. He shocks me by giving it a small shake then a kiss on my knuckles. Then he turns and shakes Malcolm's hand also before he turns and walks back through that door. As we walk back to my parents, Malcolm puts his arm around me as I put my hand in the back pocket of his scrubs. Damn, this feels so natural, I just pray once we have a much overdue conversation, we can pursue whatever the hell this is because this is the first time in a long while that I feel good. I don't want to lose this feeling or Malcolm, and I'll do whatever I can to make sure this works. For the both of us.

TWENTY-TWO
'MALCOLM'
MALTY

We sat in the waiting area until Cici was moved to the intensive care unit. First William and Sherrie went in to see their daughter. Then Frankie and I got to see her for just a few minutes. She wasn't awake, which I didn't think she'd be. I'm sure she's on some serious drugs. I know though that Frankie had to see her with her own eyes to make sure she was doing okay. Before we left, after saying our goodbyes to Cici's parents, Frankie went to the nurses' station and left her cell phone number with the nurses, telling them to call if there were any changes at all.

Now we are on our way back to the ranch. Dani is driving us in one of the club's SUVs. Not sure why, but one of the Handmaidens or Intruders will be guarding Cici's door. Also, from what Peanut told me, Sheriff George is putting a newer deputy on the rotation to keep an eye out at the hospital. My back is screaming at me and I can't wait to take a scalding hot shower to loosen some of my muscles. Then I want to sleep for like twenty-four hours.

Shamonda sent a few texts with shots of her boys and my fur babies playing. They even have the cats running all over. Thank God for them. It's not easy to leave your fur babies, so knowing they are being taken care of helps settle my nerves on being away from them. That's something else I have to think about. First though is talking things over with Frankie. I glance down to see Frankie curled up in the crook of my arm, asleep. I can't even fathom how emotionally spent she is. With us springing a surprise visit and finding out about Michael. Shit, another conversation we'll need to have. So much to try and figure out. She's worth it all though. I'd walk through hell for her. Well, we both went down that road already.

As Dani slows down, I see we are getting ready to turn onto the access road to the ranch. There are armed men at the gate, which I never noticed before. Quietly as not to disturb Frankie, I have to ask.

"Dani, I've never noticed the armed guards before? Did something happen?"

"No, Malcolm, actually since Tink's situation, we always have guards at the gates. They are either a few Intruders or some of Ollie's ex-military folks. Sometimes even Sheriff George might call in the county deputies. What we do brings us into contact with some very evil people, Malcolm. Not to mention we bring back the victims here to the ranch to heal. We've had times when our missions though successful and, in fact we rescue those being abused, but the bad people get away. We've been doing this for years, Malcolm, and we're now known for our work by the evil that walks this earth. There have been times when the ranch's weaknesses were made aware to us. When things for Tink came to a head, some very bad men made it onto the ranch and to the main house. A gunfight happened and thank God no one on our side was killed. So after that Tank, Sheriff George, and Ollie worked with Tink to secure the home front."

I feel when Frankie is starting to wake up, but just hold her tightly to me. She cuddles back into me and sighs. Not sure what that means, but she stays close, so that's all that matters to me. It's been so long since I've had this, the closeness between a man and woman. I'm not talking about the intense sexual intimacy, though I want that too again with Frankie. If I'm being honest, I want it all with her. Though that thought in itself scares the fuck out of me.

Dani stops and talks to two of the men. They are flirting with her and I don't know if she's playing hard to get or is clueless.

"She's clueless, Malty. Doesn't realize how gorgeous and nice she is."

Frankie lifts up from my body and I'm instantly cold. She stretches, which draws my eyes to her torso and breasts. She's filled out though she's petite in shape. Gorgeous is what comes to mind.

"Would you prefer a photograph so you can have it handy at all times, Malty?"

I hear Dani softly giggle as she drives down the long driveway to the ranch's main house. I look at Frankie and whisper.

"Want some company tonight?"

Her eyes get big before she grins at me.

"Dani, skip the main house. Just take us to my cabin, if you don't mind. And thanks, sister, for the ride. Appreciate it."

No one says another word in the few minutes it takes to round the main house and drive down Cabin Lane, as we've named it. Dani stops right in front of my cabin. Malcolm gets out first then reaches in for me. Before he shuts the door, I hear him say thanks to Dani, who says something though I don't catch it. I do feel Malcolm tense up for a second or two before he tells her to have a good night. We make our way up the stairs to the front door. I do the fingerprint then open the door and shut down the alarm. Once Malcolm is in, I reset it for night and two people.

"What did Dani say to you that had you tensing up?"

"She told me if I hurt you, and I thought Shadow was scary, I'd find out differently because no one would find a single piece of my body when she was done. And she said all of this with a smile on her face. Totally freaked me out, Frankie. She looks so innocent and nice."

"Malcolm, she is innocent and nice but more importantly, she's loyal. Now don't know about you, but I'm going to take a shower. Shit, you already took one at the hospital, didn't you? Well then, make yourself comfortable. I won't be long. I'm so exhausted, bet you are too. Be back."

Watching her walk down the hallway to the master bedroom, I step into her kitchen, open the refrigerator, and grab—oh yeah—an apple juice. I open the bottle and take a long drink. Damn, that is so good. I make my way back to the family room and sit down on the couch, leaning back and putting my feet without shoes on the table. Not sure how long I sit like that but the next thing I know, Frankie is back in her pajamas.

"Malcolm, come on, let's get you to bed. Do you need anything, like ice? I've got my second bedroom all ready for you. We'll talk in the morning. Hey, what are you doing? Malty, you passed my guest room. Um, this is my room. Malcolm, what are you doing?"

"Frankie, I'm too exhausted, even if you wanted to. But I do want to fall asleep with you in my arms. Promise, no hanky-panky."

She starts to laugh but surprisingly doesn't say no. I barely look at her bedroom, just walk us to the bed. She moves to one side and throws the covers back and gets in. I also move the covers and get in. Not sure how sleeping in scrubs is going to work, but at this point I just want to close my eyes and rest. With Frankie in my arms. I lie on my back and before I can shift, she's cuddled next to me, her hand across my belly. She smells so good, fresh, and kind of a mixture of fruity with flowers.

"Malty, we'll talk in the morning. I don't think I could get my brain to shoot any thoughts out of my mouth. See, that didn't even make sense. Thanks for being here."

Right before she drifts off to sleep, I could swear to all that is holy she tells me she loves me. My God, my body reacts to that in so many ways. My heart feels like it just got a jolt of electricity, my brain does a ten second reminder of what we went through, and then I promise myself to get help to move forward. My cock is throbbing and hard as steel, which shocks the shit out of me. It's been a while since it reacted at all. Well, yeah, to my hand but that is few and far between. So great time for the beast to wake up, which means I'm not going to be getting any sleep anytime soon. My hand is on Frankie's waist and just the heat of her skin feels like my hand is on fire. It could burn, not going to move it at all.

As I lie with the love of my life asleep in my arms, it dawns on me, the shit I think it was Panther was talking about: the circle of life. He was so right; we are a perfect example of that. There is so much I'm going to have to do. First item on my list after we have our talk is to reach out to Judy and have a serious chat with her too. Find out options and see how much time she's going to need from me. My condo, no, townhouse will be my next problem. I need to talk to my siblings and even Frankie's, see if anyone is looking for a home. My fur babies are in for some changes too. I worry because Buddy and Chloe are getting up in age, though both are healthy. I'm really jumping the gun here. What if my ultimate dream is not Frankie's? Better slow my ride down, I smile to myself.

As I continue to make my list, something hits me. How quiet it is out here in Bumfuck, Montana. Unlike anything I've ever experienced. I mean, for Christ's sake, I live in New York City. There is always noise, sirens, loud voices talking or shouting, kids playing, and at times even gunfire. Music is a staple of the city as are loud cars and don't forget motorcycles. I've heard some of those noises during the day but once it gets dark here, all you hear is whatever Mother Nature has planned for you and an occasional wild animal or two calling out.

Right before I start to doze, after letting my dick calm down, I say a quick thank you to the powers that be. I never in a million years thought or dreamt I be at this place with this beautiful woman in my arms. Life is a mystery, that's for fucking sure. My last thought before my brain goes to sleep is how I can't wait to make Frankie mine again. Though again I'm scared to death because I don't know how she'll react. Don't want to have the conversation on how many men she's been with either. I just want to see her gorgeous face as she lets go as her body goes limp from an orgasm. Time and time again, until she screams for me to stop. Then I'll do one more time just to see that look in her eyes and flush on her cheeks.

TWENTY-THREE
'WILDCAT'
FRANKIE

Something hard is behind me is the thought I have right before I literally jump out of my bed. Something or someone rustles the covers as I'm reaching in my nightside table to grab my gun.

"Frankie. Beautiful, it's me. Hey, Frankie, it's Malcolm. Come on, calm down. FRANKIE, IT'S MALCOLM!!!"

The last loud scream gets my attention. Shit, I plop on the side of the bed, dropping my head in my hands. What a fucked-up way to wake up, though I feel pretty rested. I grab my phone to see the time. Holy shit, it's ten o'clock in the morning, no wonder I'm rested, slept the goddamn day away. I put the phone back on the side table just as I feel the bed depress next to me and Malcolm's arms wrap around me. I put my head to his chest and take a deep breath of all that is him. The light spattering of hair on his chest with that thin line that goes to the "promised land," as I used to call it. That brings a tiny smile to my face.

"Morning, Malcolm."

"Hey, Frankie, you okay?"

"Yeah. I don't usually have someone in bed with me, so waking up feeling your rock-hard body behind me, it scared the shit out of me, and well, you see how I reacted. Thank God I didn't get to my gun and shoot you."

Malcolm just smiles down at me while pulling me even closer, if that's possible. His heat, hands, and skin wrapped all around me, I can feel my nipples getting hard and my nether land getting wet. Welp, time to move. We need to talk before we do any of that sweaty, hot sex stuff. I hear a sigh, which tells me our minds are at the same place.

"I'm going to start coffee. In the bathroom under the sink are new toothbrushes. Do you want some breakfast? Not sure about you but I'm starving. Did we eat yesterday?"

"Yes, to all of that. Remember, somebody brought in sandwiches, which someone named Momma Diane made?"

"Oh shit, that's right. And Momma Diane is Tink and Squirt's mom. Well, yeah, we can get into all of my club drama later. So eggs, bacon, and turkey sausage sound good? And I think there's still some cut-up fruit in the refrigerator too. I'll go start everything, come out when you're ready."

"Hey, Frankie, this feels not only good but right.

Though isn't usually the guy making the coffee and breakfast? How'd I get so lucky? Go, woman, start the coffee and make me some breakfast. I have spoken, wench."

Watching Malcolm fake pound on his chest brings a chuckle to my lips. Shit, this is how it could have been all these years. The love, heat, and companionship would have just kept growing between us. I mean, we could have had a toddler already if things hadn't taken a total shit on us. But we can't change the past and sure the hell don't want to drag it with me now in the present. I remember talking to Spirit from the sanctuary. Well, actually, she was walking out of the therapist's office and I was waiting to go in for a session. Our mutual therapist had to use the ladies' room so we started talking. Just from the little she revealed she's, if it's possible, more fucked up than I am. She's the one who started talking about trying to leave baggage in the past. That's when our therapist walked in and congratulated her on listening to what she told her. With that, the curtain dropped and Spirit politely said her goodbyes and left.

In the kitchen as I'm thinking about that accidental meeting, I put that on my list too. Reach out to Spirit and see how she's doing. I know Shadow has worked with her and told all of us in chapel that if Spirit wanted to become a Devil's Handmaidens sister, she'd vouch for her. And that is saying a lot. I hear Malcolm moving around in the bedroom, so I pull out cream and grab the sugar jar, placing them on the island. Then I grab two mugs, filling them with fresh coffee. I have bacon and turkey sausages in the frying pans and as I go to grab the fresh eggs from the ranch, someone is knocking on my door. Are you kidding me?

Walking to the door, I peek through the little camera thing and see Shadow. Well shit, didn't she go back to Panther's ranch last night? I open the door just as she's about to pound on it again.

"Morning, Shadow, what has you up and about this morning?"

She says nothing, just pushes her way in, walking directly to the kitchen.

"Is that coffee I'm smelling? Damn, I'd die for a cup about now. Hey, why are there two hot steaming mugs right there on the counter?"

Before I can answer, Malcolm walks out from the bedroom barefoot, jeans unbuttoned and no shirt. He has a towel around his neck and he's drying his face. Damn, I can't make this shit up. When Shadow whistles the towel drops immediately, hanging around his neck. Malcolm's eyes come first to me then to Shadow, when he grimaces. Oh, damn he didn't.

"What's the matter, Malcolm, not happy to see my smiling face after you spent the night with my sister Wildcat here? Turn around, want to see if the wildcat left marks from those nails of hers. If not then you weren't doing it right, ya know, not hitting the right 'spot.'"

She makes the finger motion when she said spot. I can't help it, between the smirk on Shadow's face and the look of disbelief on Malcolm's I snicker, then snort, and finally start to laugh. Both heads turn to me. I see Shadow's eyes narrowing, taking it all in, while Malcolm just looks flabbergasted. Then he almost brings me to my knees.

"Fuck, Frankie, never thought I'd hear that ever again. Your laughter can light up a cloudy rainy day."

Shadow's head jerks to him, then me. Then she shakes her head. When she starts to sing off-key that is when I smile her way.

"Another one bites the dust. Yeah, yeah, another one bites the dust."

Malcolm, with a huge grin on his face, joins her and together they serenade me as I cook the bacon and sausage. As I'm making the scrambled eggs, the two of them set the table. As I'm plating the food, Malcolm warms everyone's coffee as Shadow grabs ketchup and hot sauce from the fridge. We all sit and dig in. Thank God I made more than enough. As I'm shoving eggs in my mouth, it dawns on me.

"Goddamn it, I forgot to butter the toast. Hang on a second."

I get up and walk to the toaster. Pushing the bread back down I wait and in about fifteen seconds or so it pops up. Now that it's hot the butter will melt. I bring the buttered toast to the island and they each grab a piece, leaving two on the plate. This feels so good, almost like normal, whatever that means. Though I kind of know why my sister is here, I just need to confirm it.

"Shadow, not that I don't love seeing you first thing in the morning, but what's up?"

She gazes at me first then looks over to Malcolm. Something is bothering her; I can feel it.

"Need to know what you want done with Michael. Can't keep him on ice in my wet room indefinitely. Never know, might need to use that room for some actual work. Also, it's intake day so wanted to know how much you want to be involved. Usually, you are a big part of it, but I know you got a lot going on. I can try to fill your shoes but with this on my face, not going to be the calm serene shit you bring to the table."

I look to see Malcolm staring at me. Well, so much for our talk.

"Shadow, finish breakfast. Then give us about an hour or so, then we'll do whatever you want or need. As far as Michael, that's what part of that hour is for, to figure out what's next. Does that work for you?"

She just nods, though her ice-blue eyes are on Malcolm. Not a word is said but when he gives her a chin lift, I know he got what she was saying. We all go back to breakfast and before long we're done sipping our lukewarm coffees.

"Welp, better get going. Oh, Tink called a chapel for noon. Hey, did you notice I didn't give ya any bullshit for having a half-naked fine-ass man in your house? Never said a word, though when I get back to the main house, I'm gonna have to share. Need to have something good to share occasionally, otherwise all the sisters are gonna think I'm gloom and doom."

With that she throws back the last of her coffee, grabs her plate, and shit, walks it to the sink, then with a finger to the forehead walks out. Just great, everyone is going to think we were bumping nasties all night, and I didn't even get a kiss yet. Well, a real one.

"Hey, Frankie, go get ready. I'll clean up then maybe we can talk before something else happens. One thing I can say, it's never boring out here in Timber-Ghost, Montana."

With that thought in my head, I make my way back to my bedroom where the bed is made, drapes and blinds are open and up. Damn, he's good. I walk into the en suite, take one look at my hair and literally shriek. This is how I sat with Shadow and Malcolm and ate breakfast. Shit, is that why she had her phone out? Did that bitch take pictures? I'll kill her with my own two hands. Who would have thought short hair could look so frigging crazy after going to bed with wettish hair.

After working on my hair and getting dressed again, I make my way down to where I find Malcolm sitting on my couch, the television on as he's watching the news.

"Don't know how but there's no news on what happened yesterday. Nothing about Cici or anything. How can that be?"

"Welcome to small-town America, Malcolm. So think we should get this done?"

"Yeah, I do, Beautiful."

I take a few to breathe and try to think what it is I want to say to him. Over the last couple of years, I've gone back and forth with what I'd say if we ever crossed paths. Well, now that it's here, don't really know what to say or how to express what I'm feeling. I look up to see so much love on his face it instantly hits me what to say.

"Stay."

His eyes get larger and his mouth forms an "O." Then a gorgeous as fuck smile appears on his face before he pulls me close and plants a kiss on my lips. Not a touch this time, he uses his lips, teeth, and tongue to tell me what he thought of my comment. I lose track of time because the man can kiss. When he finally pulls back after multiple kisses on the tip of my nose, back to my lips, then to my forehead, I slowly open my eyes.

"Malcolm, is that a yes?"

He throws his head back belly laughing. After a second, I join him. This lasts for a bit 'til the other thing we need to talk about comes to the surface. His face gets serious before he says the one word I'm dreading.

"Michael. What are we going to do, Frankie, with him?"

At first I shrug, trying to buy some time, though I've given it some thought. Bottom line is we can't let him live. Not only because of what he did to both of us, but with his history with Shadow and her father, Dario. That brings the evil back and that can never happen. I don't say a word, just keep my eyes on him. After about five minutes or so his head drops, as his shoulders start to shake. I reach over and pull him to me. He drops his head in my lap, wraps his arms around my thighs, and lets it all out while I really feel my hatred for Michael growing.

I'll never know why he did what he did. Before we

give Shadow the go-ahead, we need to try to talk to him for some kind of closure. Especially for Malcolm. As my hands run through his hair, I can't believe that we both want the same thing. Us together. Miracles do happen... look at the two of us. Now for the hard stuff, this ain't going to be easy but with Malcolm at my side I feel we can do anything together.

TWENTY-FOUR
'WILDCAT'
FRANKIE

Sitting in our meeting room at the ranch, I'm waiting like everyone else for Tink and Glory to arrive. This is very strange; they are never late. Next to me is Heartbreaker. I lean over, shoulder bumping her.

"You did good yesterday, sister, with Cici. Thanks for that, so much was happening I'm glad she had someone there for her. From what Shadow told us this morning at breakfast, Cici's up though still pretty groggy. We're going to try and see her today if you want to come with us."

She looks at me for a second then smiles, which shocks me. Damn, never realized how gorgeous this sister is.

"Um, Wildcat, who's we and why didn't I get an invite to breakfast?"

Someone with eagle ears puts in her two cents.

"I didn't get one either, Heartbreaker. Think I broke up a little personal breakfast party. I mean, damn,

Malcolm is one fine piece of meat, if I say so myself, though not as good as my Panther."

Fuck, she did it, the bitch. And with the room full. Every eye is on me as I feel my face flush. Before I can say anything, the doors open and in walk Tink, Glory, and Dr. Cora. That's strange, is one of them sick or something?

"Shit, sorry we're late, got caught up in our conversation. We're going to start with something not on the schedule. Everyone knows Dr. Cora; she's been a part of us forever. No, don't get your panties in a bunch, she's still going to be a part of us, wrong choice of words."

My eyes search out Shadow because our prez never mixes her words up. She's always on top of it in meetings or conference calls. Even that time when that special FBI person called for help and Tink walked him through our process. Something is definitely up when Shadow gives me big eyes.

"Okay, so Glory, Cora, and I had a meeting this morning that Cora wanted. Turns out our doc has been keeping some secrets from us. Well, I'll let her tell you."

Cora looks at Tink with a look that says *are you crazy*. Tink just grins, her green eyes twinkling, though there is some sadness in them. *Wonder why?* I think to myself. Then Cora actually stands and looks at all of us.

"Damn it, Tink, put me on the spot. All right, shit, some of you know this and others probably don't. What you all do is beyond courageous and so needed in our country—nope—world. For women who aren't professionally trained to take on the evil and demons who walk this earth, I had to be a part of it. And the reason I needed to is because many years ago, when I was just a kid, a man and woman grabbed me from a park."

She looks right at Squirt, a very small smile on her face.

"Yeah, Squirt, told you I understood. Didn't tell you because that time was about you not me. Anyhow, they kept me for years or until I was an almost fifteen. Then a new girl appeared and I knew my time was coming to an end. One day, when they weren't paying attention, I escaped and ran. I ran so hard and fast, thought I was gonna die. Came upon a small little farm with a mom and a few kids. Long story short, her husband died in a freak accident. She hid me. And that couple came to her farm lying, saying their daughter ran away and they were so worried. Only problem is, Annie saw the scars and listened to my story. If not for that one woman taking a chance, risking her family for me, I'd not be standing in front of you."

She reaches for the travel mug she brought in and takes a drink.

"Annie is suffering with Alzheimer's and it's getting worse. We've obviously kept in touch as I consider her like a second mom and her three kids as my siblings. Oh, forgot to add my parents wanted nothing to do with me when I finally reached out so Annie became my parent, though not legally. I haven't spoken to my parents since I was sixteen. I was going to move to Great Falls to help take care of Annie but my sister, Linda, suggested maybe bringing Mom out to me. Well, the long and short of it is, not only is Annie relocating but so are the two younger kids. Well, young adults. My older sister is a Marine and is overseas in Fallujah. Now that I've regurgitated part of my life story on y'all, I'm going to be stepping back from some of my duties here, and I'm truly sorry. I can't let this woman suffer alone. My sister and brother are barely adults and can't handle this progressive disease. My older sister, Marty, can't get out of the Marines. She has six months left then she'll be coming back to the States. We've talked and she said there's nothing for her in Great Falls and Timber-Ghost sounds like a good place to start again. She's interested in what y'all do, so maybe a new prospect, who knows. Anyway, Tink has been generous enough to sell to me that little building next to the east horse pasture. Well, she did that a while ago. Ollie and some of his folks have been remodeling it and getting it ready for Annie. I can't take care of my family and still manage this family; it wouldn't be fair to any of you. So I'll still be around, obviously, but in a more part-time fashion. For the clinic, Tink and Glory are looking for a replacement. I'll be on a rotation to be their backup and if you bring home large groups of victims, I definitely will help with that. All I ask is that you all come visit. Make Annie's last days brighter and joyful."

Cora sits down softly crying. Glory reaches for her when what Doc just said penetrates my brain. My eyes shoot to Tink, who's watching me with those green eyes that see everything. In a brief second it dawns on me what this woman just did. I don't know what to do until Tink mouths, "Just breathe."

After Cora answers a few questions she leaves, and Glory starts the meeting. I actually have no idea what was discussed until I am called about the intake today.

Glory has to call my name a few times to get my attention.

"Yeah, sorry, Glory, trying to get my brain to catch up. I'm planning on being there during the intake. I think we have around what... thirteen or maybe a few more? Saying that, it's going to be a long couple of days. I know the therapist at the Blue Sky Sanctuary will be on hand, as will Dr. Cora, I think."

Tink raises her hand to stop me.

"Yeah, Wildcat, she will be. Maybe ask Malcolm to come with you so he can get an idea of what happens after a mission. He works the emergency room, right? So he's used to on-the-spot medical treatment. He did very good with Cici from what Yoggie told Noodles."

After about another thirty or forty minutes Tink calls the meeting and everyone stands to leave. Shadow calls out my name to hang for a bit, so I sit back down. Tink, Shadow, and Glory come my way as Rebel shuts the doors and sits right next to me. Goddamn, I forgot how ripped she is. Between her and Raven I feel like a little kid, can't imagine what Tink feels like as she's smaller than me.

"I know we kinda talked about it at breakfast, but did you and Malcolm have words over what's next for

Michael? Wildcat, gotta say if I have a vote, I want him gone and I mean forever. I can't talk about it but there is shit that's happened between him, my father, and me that fucked me up. I mean, well anyway, that's all I got."

They all wait to see what I'm going to say. No one rushes me at all, which gives me a second to gather my thoughts before I say what needs to be said.

"Malcolm and I did talk about Michael. Between the four of you and these walls it's devastated him, all that he's found out about his best friend. Saying that, we both know he can't leave the ranch, or well, the clubhouse wet room, whichever he ends up at."

Rebel leans over to me.

"Wildcat, he's here. Transferred him myself early this morning. He's in the far barn in the secret room. No worries, he's still breathing."

They had already decided what was going to happen but wanted to give me a chance to voice Malcolm's and my opinions. Well, here goes.

"There is one thing we both want. Well, two, I guess. First, we want to talk to him alone. No, let me finish. I'm not sure he'd be honest with someone else in the room. Second, and this is the most important for Malcolm, he doesn't want him to die alone. Yeah, I get it, Shadow, but try and see his point of view. They grew up together, became adults, and share so many experiences. If I can, I've got to give this to him. We don't want to watch you work, just call us when it's time, that's all."

Tink looks to Shadow and they do that thing just like Panther and Avalanche. Though these two women have been doing this as long as I've known them. Tink nods and Shadow looks down my way.

"Okay to the second request, though for the first both Rebel and I will be in there. No, hear me out now. If he gets mouthy or downright ignorant, neither you nor Malcolm will want to do anything to shut him up. The two of us have no personal relationship with him so we are your backup. That's all, I don't care for the filth he spills. Do what you must for your ol' man, Wildcat, but let your sisters have your back, that's all I'm sayin'."

Three sets of eyes are on me but Glory is the one who asks the question.

"Your ol' man? Since when does Wildcat have an old man, and who the fuck is it...wait, I'm slow today. Do you mean Malcolm, Shadow? Holy shit, how—no—when did this happen?"

"About give or take fifteen plus years ago. Yeah, we're a work in progress and big mouth over there hasn't given me a chance to share."

This starts another conversation, so by the time I answer all the questions it's another thirty or so minutes. When everyone gets up to leave, Tink asks me to hang back for a minute. When they are all gone, she motions for me to come closer.

"I knew from the moment I saw the two of you together the end result is what I just heard. So after much thought and some talking it over with Noodles, knew that I had to find a way to keep the both of you here where you belong. Sorry, Wildcat, but your home isn't New York anymore, it's here at the ranch. And no, I didn't push Dr. Cora out. That door just closed a bit and then opened for Malcolm. We've not asked him yet and not sure he'll be interested. Time will tell. Know this, sister, no matter where you go or what you do, this will always be home. And your folks, sisters, and brother are welcome anytime. My job as your president, and more importantly your sister, is to take care of you and that's what I'm trying to do. Please don't take offense."

I don't say a word, just stand up and pull her into me, hugging her tightly. They broke the mold when God made her. And this world is a luckier place because she's in it. After a bit we separate, then I smile before I turn and head toward where the intake is going on. I grab my phone and tell Malcolm to meet me at the first bunkhouse whenever he can get there. Also tell him to let my folks know I'll be busy most of the day. Then I take the rest of the walk to get my head in the right place to help these women face a new day. The first one in their new lives.

TWENTY-FIVE
'MALCOLM'
MALTY

If someone would have told me years ago this would be my life, I would have cracked up. But here I am on a ranch in Montana. Nope, haven't gotten on a horse yet, which is pissing both Panther and Avalanche off. Oh well, can't be perfect all the time.

Those two men are quickly becoming my friends. With that word in my head, it brings to mind another friend I used to have, or so I thought. I never knew how messed up Michael was. When Frankie told me we got the okay to speak to him semi-privately, it actually scared me, but I did it and I'm glad I did. It kind of gave me closure.

He wasn't really thrilled about it, especially with Shadow and Rebel in the room, but true to their words they sat in the farthest corner on their phones unless he acted like an asshole. And he did a few times but after his last toenail was pulled out, he kinda mellowed out. Frankie didn't ask him anything, though he spewed all kinds of shit her way until I screamed stop. Then I asked the one question I needed an answer to.

"Why?"

His head jerks back. They have him tied arms, legs, hands, and feet to a chair. He is in nothing but his boxer briefs. His body is covered in bruises—some old, some new. You can tell which are which by the coloring. His lip is split and one eye is black and blue. Some of his fingers are broken and I'm sure he has internal issues also. I don't ask anything about that. I want to know why. And what he shares knocks me on my ass.

"What do you mean **why,** Malcolm? Are you trying to tell me you don't know? Come on, after all of this and the years we've been together."

Whoa wait, the years we've been together? What the fuck, he's talking like a past lover of mine. Then it hits me like a frying pan to the head. He doesn't give me a chance as he keeps babbling.

"You never truly noticed me. The real me, Malcolm. Let me refresh your memory *'friend.'* I think it was eighth grade or ninth, not sure. That party we went to where they had whiskey and weed. We tried both together. Got totally wasted and ended up downstairs on the couch. You put your hand on my thigh while we were talking and I just knew then. So I got on my knees opened your jeans and grabbed your cock. I'd never done it before, even if it was my best fantasy. I took your cock and licked it before I sucked it into my mouth. You didn't stop me or even push me away. You let me give you a blow job and right before the big finish, just as you were shooting your cum down my throat, you destroyed me when you whispered, 'Yeah, Frankie, just like that. *Take it, Beautiful, take all of me.*' When you reached out the next day to talk about it, letting me know that though it happened you were drunk and high but it wouldn't ever again, and you didn't want it to become a problem between us. You then told me how Frankie was the one for you and you were sorry about what happened. I laughed it off and even told you that she didn't need to know because it was a one and done. We continued our friendship, or that's what I let you think. Years, Malcolm, I waited, planned, did whatever I had to. Made connections with the worst of the worst, sucked so many dicks I lost count. Even let the freak Dario fuck me up the ass. It helped me plan that day. The day I'd dreamed about forever.

"Joey and Gerald were losers of Dario's but did whatever I told them for drugs. Buck was a redneck who didn't particularly like takin' orders from someone of my skin color, if you know what I mean. Frankie, bet he's burning in hell fuming that a woman of mixed heritage took him out. Didn't think it would go down the way it did. I wanted you to know it was me, Malcolm, but by the time I arrived you were beat to hell, almost dead because those stupid fuckers were high and lost control. That didn't stop me. I'd waited my entire life for that moment. Gerald ripped your pants down and I finally found Heaven on earth. When that bitch opened the door, I saw the cherry on the sundae, so to speak. Told Joey to grab her and keep her in the house. I enjoyed you thoroughly, Malcolm, because I knew it was gonna have to last me the rest of my life. You bitch, it was all about doing the most damage I possibly could. After I finished, I grabbed that vase and gave it my all. To my surprise you not only survived but recovered, while Malcolm here suffered through multiple surgeries and shit bags. And I was there to get him over every setback. Now let me guess, you two are back together. The Malcolm/Frankie show is taking prime time and I sit here while that other crazy as fuck bitch ends my life. Yeah, I know where this is going, not stupid. Hope I gave you what you needed to hear, Malcolm, to move on with your life and forget me."

Michael smirks at me while I'm trying to process what he just said. I move closer and Shadow jumps up, moving right off to my side. She gives me a look I'll never forget.

"You stupid motherfucker. I loved you like my own brother. I took you in, cared for you. Fuck, yeah, we had a moment when we were kids. Michael, most people experiment in their lives to figure out who they are supposed to be. Why didn't you just come and talk to me? No, I wouldn't have changed my mind but we could have tried to work it out. You wasted your life for nothing. I feel sorry for you, Michael. Wasting your entire life in anger, wanting revenge because of a demented dream you tried to force on me. My God, man, you could have had the world at your feet. Instead, you're facing imminent death by the hands of another person you've fucked over. Thanks for the honesty and closure, brother. I'd wish you well, but it doesn't even matter."

"Malcolm, don't leave me. Come on, we can get over this. Don't leave, motherfucker. I did it all for you."

Standing, I walk over to where my once best friend is tied to a chair. I lean down and whisper in his ear.

"I loved you, Michael. Wanted you to be my best man at my wedding, godfather to my children. Grow old, drinking beer, watching the games on a huge screen television. No, what's happening is all on you."

Then I walk out of the room with tears running down my face as I start to mourn my best friend.

* * *

The next morning at five, Frankie's phone rings. She reaches for it and answers. In less than five seconds she looks at me then says, "Yeah, we'll be there in a few. Thanks, sister."

Then she pulls me close and whispers, "It's time."

Together we get up and get dressed. When I tell Frankie I need a minute or two she goes to make us some coffee. I shut the bathroom door, sit on the toilet, and let all the sorrow I'm feeling out. My God, how am I supposed to watch the one person besides Frankie I thought would always have my back die? Like I told Michael yesterday, be the godfather to my kids, if I had them, my best man at my wedding first. Fuck, it's tearing my heart out. When I open the door, I actually scream like a little girl. Panther and Avalanche are both sitting on the bed. They stand when I come out. Panther comes toward me, putting his hands on my shoulders.

"We're here for ya, brother. Been in touch with Zoey throughout the night and just so you know, it's killing her. Rebel has done most of it because Zoey thinks you're going to hate her. No matter how badass she tries to play, she has a tender heart. What do you need, Malcolm?"

"I need this shit done and behind us. What I want is to have the person I thought was my best friend back and not being about to hold hands when he dies. This is what I have, so guess just going to do my best."

They start for the kitchen with me behind them. I stop dead in my tracks when I see Billie and Enzo sitting at the counter. When she sees me, Billie immediately walks to me, pulling me close, telling me she's here for me. That they are my family. Son of a bitch. Enzo is right behind her and when he pulls me close, that's it. My shoulders start to shake and he just holds on to me tighter. When I feel like I can function, I pull away. Frankie is right there when her dad moves away from me.

Avalanche comes toward me with a huge feather and a bunch of something burning. When I look to Frankie, her eyes are on the big man. I'm guessing this is something important from the way she's watching him.

"Malcolm, in our culture, when an important event happens in one's life we smudge. Today for you is not only important but heavy and sad. Smudging cleanses you or wherever you are. Before you face your friend, I want you protected. Taz said I forget if it was her or Teddy who gave you a crystal. Carry that with you. This will only take a minute or two, then we go. I need you to close your eyes and try to remember a happy time with Michael. Before your attack when you were together as brothers. That's it, take a few deep breaths and slowly release. Keep those memories in your mind's eye and when you go into that room, pull that moment up. If necessary, remind him of it. That might help him pass without a heavy heart."

Opening my eyes, I see he's swiping the smoke with the feather toward me. He goes up and down my body, front and back, then steps away. Everyone is quiet as he extinguishes what I now know is white sage. Panther and Avalanche each take a side and lead me out the cabin and toward the barn where Michael is being held. I can feel Frankie at my back with Enzo and Billie following behind her. Not a long walk but when we turn toward the last barn, I lose it. The women of the Devil's Handmaidens are all there leaning against the two barns on either side. No one says a word or even approaches me, but knowing they are there not just for Frankie, but maybe me too gives me some strength.

At the door we stop. Both men squeeze my shoulder then move away. I see Panther on his phone just as Frankie grabs my hand and squeezes. Within a minute or two both Shadow and Rebel come out. Both are exhausted, but Shadow looks much worse than Rebel. As Shadow goes to Panther, Rebel moves closer to us.

"He was rough on her. Brought up a lot of shit from

her past that he was involved with. We'll go through everything but, Malcolm, he never went away to college. That was when he hooked his star to Dario De Luca. In the end, she couldn't even get close to him. So, if you get pissed at someone it's me, not her. You both can go in. No, I cleaned him up best I could. We'll follow, you know why. Whenever you're ready and for what it's worth, Malcolm, Wildcat, I'm sorry it ended up like this. Just so you know, Malcolm, no matter what, this club always comes first."

Rebel walks away to stand next to Shadow, whose eyes are down. Malcolm moves to go in and I'm right with him. We walk in and take the first left then a right. This room was renovated just for Shadow and her work. This is the room she roughed up Heartbreaker in. The door is pulled but not latched closed. I can smell the bleach and not sure... Lysol? I'm the one who pushes the door open and we both gasp. Not what I was expecting. Michael is on a type of hospital bed an IV in his one arm. He's under covers. If you didn't know better, you'd think you were in a hospital. Walking slowly to the bed, when I get within reach, I gently touch what I think is his arm. At first nothing, but when I do it again his eyes seem to struggle to open. At first, it's like he's blind but after some time he focuses and sees me. His lips form a slight smile, well, until he sees Frankie. The hatred in his eyes strengthens my spine. We both made our choices though mine never intentionally hurt anyone, unlike his.

"Michael, if you will let me, I'll stay with you. Don't want you to be by yourself. No matter what we've been through, family stays together, Michael, and you're my family."

"Yeah, I know, Malcolm, I'm your family from your past…your brother. Frankie's your future. Believe me, that's been punched and poked into me."

He starts to cough and blood and clots cover the blanket. Immediately Rebel comes over with another blanket, removing the bloody one and putting the clean one on. Michael is in what looks like men's pajamas. I look to Frankie then the chair right off to the side of the one next to Michael. She totally understands as she squeezes my hand then goes and sits in the chair. I also take the seat by my friend's bed. When I go to grab his hand, it takes me a startled second to realize he's missing his fingers. Oh, holy fuck, what did they do to him? I'm up in a second but before I can rip the blanket off him, Shadow is standing on the other side, her hand on the blanket holding it to Michael's chest. He looks to be squirming but that could be my imagination.

"Malcolm, don't go looking for trouble. What's done is done. You are here to support your brother. We will stay out of your way, just don't cross that line. Please trust me."

The look in those icy-blue eyes tells me to drop it. When I sit back down, she moves back to the wall, leaning against it with one foot up on it. Michael watches our interaction but says nothing.

Time goes by and it's mostly quiet, but there are times Michael wants to talk. About two hours in, Rebel comes close and that's when I see that he is catheterized.

She is checking his output, which was brownish red. His kidneys are done. *It won't be long,* I think to myself. Rebel confirms it when she looks my way.

It's now or never. I stand up and lean down to Michael so he can see me.

"Hey, Michael, look at me. Can you see me? I want you to know even though I don't understand why, I forgive you. I've loved you almost all my life and I'm so sorry it wasn't the way you wanted. You need to know there are all kinds of love, and you have one and Frankie has another. I know you wanted what she has, but deep down you knew it wasn't going to happen. I wish you would have talked to me but that's neither here nor there. I want you to leave with some kind of peace."

Tears are coming from his eyes. Goddamn, this is harder than I thought. He clears his throat, and I almost pass the fuck out when Shadow brings a cup of water with a straw. Michael watches her, fear in his eyes, but she just motions for him to drink. Once he's taken a few small sips he's able to talk some.

"Malcolm, you are a sap. No, I mean that in the best way. I'd never forgive you if our roles were reversed. Tell Frankie to come up here, please. Hurry, Malcolm, don't have a lot of time."

I motion for her to come next to me. We hold hands and look down at Michael to see he's looking at our hands. Then he looks up at us.

"Do me one favor, Frankie. Give him the life he deserves and once this is over, forget I ever existed. Malcolm, sick or not, I've loved you my entire adult life and not the brotherly love. Now my terror ends. Be happy, both of you."

When his eyes close, I look to Shadow.

"No, he's still here, though the morphine he drank with his water should slowly slow his heart and he will go peacefully. I did that for both of you, not for him."

With that I watch Shadow and Rebel leave. And five minutes later Michael leaves too, permanently.

TWENTY-SIX
'WILDCAT'
FRANKIE

It's been two and a half weeks since Michael passed away. There was no funeral or graveside burial. His body was removed, and I have no idea what they did with it. Neither Malcolm nor I want to know, though a few days after he died Teddy and Olivia wanted us to come to their home.

When we show up, I can tell something is up. Enforcer pulls me over to tell me their dog, Tuna, isn't doing good at all. Teddy and Olivia come out holding hands, as usual, but Teddy's eyes are red. Taz follows her son with the same red eyes. Not wanting to intrude, we ask what Teddy wants us here for. We walk to their new garden area in the back of their house. Off to the side is a small bush or maybe, I guess, it's a seedling.

"Malcolm, your momma told us you lost a friend and you are sad. I'm sorry for your loss. Dad helped me pick it out and plant it. It's called the Michael Rose. So, when you're sad, you can come out here, sit in the chair we put there, and talk to your friend. I hope it helps."

That's when Malcolm totally loses it. He bends down, picks Teddy up, and walks to the chair, sitting in it. Malcolm has no idea the boy is autistic but for some reason Teddy doesn't fight. He pats Malcolm's cheeks. Olivia walks over and sits at Malcolm's knees. I turn to see Taz in Enforcer's arms. He just gives me a nod and walks her into the house. Wanting to go to Malcolm at the same time I want to comfort Taz, I let my gut tell me where to go and I'm so happy I do. Taz is in their great room, somehow on the floor, Tuna's head in her lap. Enforcer is almost lying next to the once big dog. One of the vets from the sanctuary is messing with filling some syringes. Oh, dear God, this is going to kill Taz, Teddy, and from the looks of it, Enforcer. The two German shepherds are off in the corner, their eyes on their sister, Tuna.

I feel like I'm intruding until Taz lifts her head, sees me, and puts her hand out. Immediately I walk to her, get down on my knees, then fall to my ass so I can be next to her.

"Goddamn, Wildcat, why does this hurt more than when you lose a person? We haven't had her that long and my heart feels like it's being pulled right from my chest."

I glance at Tuna, who has her eyes on her daddy. He's whispering to her which seems to calm her, though she's never been a nervous dog. Stoic. There are crystals surrounding Tuna on her bed. I smell the same scent Avalanche used on Malcolm the day Michael died. I don't know what to do, so I grab on to Taz. The vet comes over and asks if they are ready. Enforcer pushes up, wiping his face.

"What do you think, man, do we look fuckin' ready? Just do it."

Then he leans back down and cuddles with his dog. That's when I see Taz has her phone out just as she snaps a shot of her husband with their first fur baby. The vet says not a word about Enforcer's outburst. He proceeds to start an IV. Once in, he sits on his heels.

"Enforcer, Taz, the first shot I'm going to give Tuna is to relax her. It'll be like she's sleeping. The second one will slow her heart until it stops. I'm going to give her the relaxer then the second shot. Here we go."

Never in my life have I been present when this was done. There is no way in heaven or hell that Tuna doesn't know she is loved. Her parents are with her the entire time. When she is gone, the vet picks up all his supplies and garbage.

"I'm very sorry for your loss. When you are ready, please let me know. I'll load Tuna up in my truck and will take her to the crematory. I'll personally return her when everything has been done. Do you want an imprint of her paw?"

Both Taz and Enforcer nod but no words. Taz is now on the sectional above Tuna as Enforcer lifted her up and put her there. Just as the vet goes to leave, we hear their screen door open and the kids and Malcolm walk in. Teddy instantly takes in the scene and goes completely still. Olivia gets closer to him, but the boy only has eyes for his dog.

"Momma, is she gone? Did she cross over to the Rainbow Bridge?"

Taz nods as Enforcer moves to go to his son, but Teddy runs straight to Tuna. Lying right next to her, he starts to cry while petting her, telling her how much he loves her. He promises never to forget her. Somehow the pups feel the vibe and slowly make their way to Tuna and Teddy. One lies next to Tuna, the other next to Teddy. Again, I see Taz with her phone out snapping a shot.

Malcolm grabs my hand, pulling me out of the room, giving the family some time. Not even five minutes later Taz comes waddling out. She gives Malcolm a small tight smile but comes directly to me.

"Thanks, sister. We knew it was time, but were afraid how Teddy would take it. As you can see, all around that rose bush are petunias. His way of letting us know he was ready. Don't feel like you have to stay, you did something I'll never be able to thank you for. Love ya, Wildcat."

She kisses my cheek, grabs on to Malcolm's arm, then walks back to her family. We get back in our vehicle and head back to the cabin. This is not the way I thought today would go. Tomorrow Malcolm is heading back to New York. Lots has happened since he said goodbye to his friend. We've gotten to know each other again. And as I keep telling Shadow no, we've not had sex, and only God knows if we ever will. Though from the look and feel of it, we will when the time is right. Yeah, I love him, but once you're violated things are different. He feels the same. We've experimented with our limits and for now we're good where we are at. We need time and that's exactly what we'll have. Malcolm is going back to New York to give his notice, though he's already spoken to Judy. He's working with Shamonda, who's going to buy his townhouse. He's giving a lot of his stuff to my brother for his new place.

Once everything is completed, I'm going to fly out to New York for the first time since I left to drive back to Montana with him. Well, with Malcolm, Buddy, Chloe, Peanut, Buttons, and China. What a cluster, but it's my clusterfuck and I love it.

"Sorry, babe, didn't know that was going down. It was nice what the kids did for you. Think it helped little Teddy more than you. He adored Tuna. Why is life so hard sometimes?'

Malcolm reaches over and grabs my hand. Then he gives it to me like he always does, honest and to the point.

"Frankie, if life wasn't hard at times when the easy ones come, we wouldn't appreciate them. As hard for Teddy and his family as that is, they have good memories with Tuna 'til she—shit, what is it called, yeah —crossed the Rainbow Bridge. Now let's take a drive before we go back to the cabin. Something I want to show you that Avalanche shared with me a while ago."

We drive for less than ten minutes. Malcolm parks my Tahoe, turns it off, and turns to me.

"Trust me, Frankie?"

"Always, Malty."

He smiles, gets out, and comes around to my door. Once we are both out, I see some sticks in the ground with string or rope strung from one to the other. What the hell, this is part of Tink's ranch.

"Damn, going to have to let Tink know someone's out here fucking with her land."

"Don't worry, she knows. And it isn't her land, it's ours. Frankie Camano, let's build our forever home here in the middle of Bumfuck, Montana. Now that I'm an employee of the Devil's Handmaidens and Blue Sky Sanctuary, figured I need to find somewhere close to live. Talked to Tink and Noodles about some land. She told me to pick a spot and it was ours, so I asked Avalanche for his help. This land is fertile if we want to have a garden, large enough if we want to add our pack of fur babies and has the most gorgeous dawns and sunsets."

I'm in his arms before I can say a word. This is what was missing in my life. My Malty. Now everything is how it should be in my life.

* * *

Want more Wildcat and Malcolm?

Goto https://dl.bookfunnel.com/8o5zhjabsd *to download a bonus epilogue.*

* * *

Rebel, Book Eight
'REBEL'
Myra

Damn, these women are driving me bat-ass crazy. Yeah, I'm part owner of the Handmaidens Fitness & Holistic Center. My partner, or should I say since Raven's kidnapping and getting shot, she reached out to me to see if I wanted to maybe get involved in the gym. We've been going over the logistics of her bringing me on as a partner, but she already has a silent partner in our prez, Tink. She was all for Raven starting this club. Our prez likes, as she puts it, "the Handmaidens to have their hands in everything." So now I'm going to be a business owner along with Raven and, I guess, Tink too. Good thing is I don't have to have a huge amount of cash to buy in. Our prez handles all the financials in every business the club is involved with. Helps our sisters find work and supports our town with businesses and jobs also.

Then last year, when Taz came to Raven and me after all the shit that went down with Raven, we talked it out and added the holistic section to the center. There isn't much I wouldn't do for Taz. Fuck, when all her drama hit, I lost my fucking mind. She's not my blood sister, but she means more than both of those bitches I share blood with. Then the whole thing with her hooking her star to Enforcer took me by surprise, but it works for them and that's all that matters.

Taz and Enforcer's family are having a rough time and I'm trying to be as supportive as they'll let me. After a battle with cancer they lost their pitbull, Pituynia, or as we all called her Tuna. Little Teddy is devastated but I'm more worried about Taz. She's pregnant, ready to drop any day, and she doesn't need the added stress. Since Tuna passed, she's not been in here and is hanging out by herself in their new home. Enforcer texted me yesterday to tell me that his Que, which is his nickname for my sister Taz, kicked him out of their house. He's also beside himself. Right now, I have to deal with these members who think I owe them every single damn minute of my time. The one giving me the hardest time is a young woman named Cleo. She had a baby almost a year ago, and she's pissed her two days a week gossip session hasn't given her the body she wants. I don't fucking know, but the actress photo she showed me when she joined is never gonna happen. And I honestly told her that. I just had a fifteen-minute conversation with her, trying once again to explain that two-thirty minute sessions of exercise are not going to remove extra weight if she's not controlling her food intake. I didn't mention out of those thirty minutes, she's probably only exercising maybe half the time. She got really pissed at me, telling me she lives on salads, fruits, and protein. Personally, I know she's lying, because Peanut, who works at our bar and grill in town, told me she's there a few times a week either stuffing her face or guzzling wine like there's no tomorrow. Not my business but one thing I can't stand is someone who lies. So, in a roundabout way, I brought it up and she immediately told me she was quitting, and that I'm just a queer-ass bitch who's probably on steroids and can't catch a man. Okay, good morning to me.

Hearing the doorbells chiming, I walk to the front of the building to see Taz waddling in. She's got a bag in one hand and her oversized purse in the other, while her pregnant tummy is sticking out in front of her. With her rainbow hair and all her crystals, she's such a sight to see. So truly unique you have to love her and her free spirit.

'What the hell are you doing here, Taz? Thought the doc said you were to take it easy, feet up? Please tell me you didn't drive yourself."

"Well, hello to you too, Rebel. Nice way to greet your best friend and godchild who's not here yet. Crap, thought I'd catch a break at least here. Want to use the meditation room to manifest my baby being born, maybe then the little one will come finally."

Smiling, I walk toward her, grabbing the bag. It's pretty heavy, and before looking in it, I know it's filled with her crystals and other shit. I don't understand any of the crystal stuff or the meanings, but I love her so much, I try to respect her ways. I noticed her face is flushed so when she tries to grab her belly in a sneaky way that I wouldn't think anything of it, my gut tightens.

"Fuck, Taz! Sister, are you in labor?"

Her head flings up and, by the look in those big, beautiful eyes, I don't need a verbal answer from her. Reaching for my phone, I go to text Enforcer when suddenly my phone goes flying from her hitting it out of my hand.

"What in the ever-lovin' fuck, Taz? We need to let people know so you can go to the hospital."

"No, Rebel, you are going to help me set up the meditation room so I can have my baby here in serenity and peace. I don't want the sterile environment of a hospital welcoming my baby. It's bad vibes, and you know that means the world to me. This baby needs to come into the world naturally, without strangers all around."

Is she goddamn nuts? For Pete's sake she's been ranting about having the baby in a bathtub. Enforcer is totally against it. Oh shit, what the fuck? Did she come here to try and drag that steel tub we use for cryotherapy from the back to have her baby in? And then what... after she kills herself dragging it into her meditation room, then she tries to fill it between contractions? Then, I guess, soak for a bit, and I don't know, push out her goddamn baby with no pain meds by herself. HERE. In my gym, while it's open and folks are working out or taking classes. Holy shit, no way in God's name is that happening here. I'm no doula, which is what Taz looked for but couldn't find in Bumfuck,

Montana. I can't handle this, no way. What if something goes wrong? Oh God, that would kill me if something happened to Taz or the lil' peanut.

"Taz, no way in hell am I letting you do this. It's not safe or even sterile here. That baby needs to be given the best chance when it's born. Think, sister, we can take some of your crystal shit to the hospital."

Before she can reply, she leans forward then doubles over, letting out a loud groan of pain. I mean, it sounds like she's in intense pain. Shit, she's not just going into labor; she's having full-blown contractions. Since I've been her second coach in the Lamaze classes, I know we need to get her to try and relax and breathe through each contraction. We have to time how far apart they are too. First, I need to know how she got here.

"How the hell did you get here, Taz? If you tell me you drove yourself, when you're done giving birth to my godchild I'm gonna kick your ass before I kill you. Jesus Christ, what are you thinking?"

She starts to giggle then, holy shit, lets out a loud as fuck fart and doubles over again. The stench is killing me, though I'm trying to be a good best friend and not to say anything.

"Damn, Travis is right, those pregnancy farts really stink. Shit, Rebel it hurts so frigging bad. Damn, how did I do this with Teddy? I can't remember everything but I don't think it was this bad, though I had drugs back then."

I know we're in trouble because she doesn't swear all that often. I grab her arm and walk her to the room in question. Off to the one side is a smaller room for massage. I turn the light on, pull the weighted blanket off the table, grab a sheet, flip it open and on the bed, then lower it as far as it will go. I grab her purse, throwing it on the floor next to her bag of crystals. She waddles to me trying to bend for that bag.

"What do you want, Taz? Need you to get on that bed now."

"No, I want a water birth, you know that. It's better and more relaxing for me and the baby. Travis is against it, but that's what I want. Oh, forgot to tell you I didn't drive here, I called an Uber."

I knew bringing that modern-ass shit to our town was gonna cause trouble, though it helps folks make a living, sort of. Whoever picked up Taz doesn't have a clue how much trouble they are going to be in. Enforcer is gonna lose his fucking mind. And whoever was supposed to be on Taz duty will be getting an ass kicking from me. Told Tink that shit wouldn't work. We should have put both pregnant sisters together in a safe room. Don't care how crazy that sounds, at least we'd have eyes on them twenty-four seven.

Looking up, I see my bestie watching me with sweat on her forehead. She's pulling her rainbow hair up with a scrunchy. Damn, why can't I tell her no?

"Swear to Christ, Taz, you're lucky I love your rainbow ass. I'll go grab that big metal pool thing we use out in the back room. Gonna take me a minute or two so just breathe and try to relax. Oh yeah, text your ol' man and tell him what's going on right now."

With that I walk out, leaving the door open. When out of sight, I start to jog while pulling my phone out. I text Tink, Shadow, and Glory with a SOS then the words "Taz is in heavy labor at our gym. Need HELP."

Not paying attention, I plow into something hard and extremely huge. I drop my phone and when I go to reach down for it, my head hits something that feels like either a large boulder or maybe a bowling ball. It literally knocks me to my knees as I hear a deep gravelly voice saying, "What the motherfucking shit? Damn, woman, watch where you're going. Oh shit, are you okay? Hey, can you hear me?"

Trying to open my eyes, I feel like I was hit by a frigging freight train. Slowly I pry my eyelids up and see the most beautiful eyes I've ever seen in a scowl that makes Enforcer's and Shadow's look like a grin. Dark brown hair with just a slight scattering of gray at the sides. Those eyes are like a caramel with rings of gold and green around the pupils. He's leaning over me, literally shaking me by the shoulders.

"Hey, you trying to finish the job, you asshole? Never heard of Shaken Adult Syndrome. Let go of me before I seriously hurt you. I said, get your hands off me."

He leans his ass onto his calves, never taking his eyes off me, though with my words a sexy grin appears on his face as his eyes sparkle. Oh, one of those types. Just what I need, a confident, built, hot motherfucker in my gym. I don't recognize him, but kind of remember my part-timer telling me we had a hottie join the club. This must be him. Great way to meet, though he's good on my eyes, for sure.

"Just checking to make sure you're okay. Took a pretty bad hit when we knocked heads."

"No, you mean when not only did you plow into me, but instead of stepping back, you rammed me with that enormous ninepin you call a head."

His face tightens as his eyes narrow at me. Whatever. Just as I remember my sister, Taz, and what I was about to do I hear tiny footsteps coming our way. Before I can turn my head, I hear the Mickey Mouse voices of young children.

"Daddy, hurry a lawy is in pwain. Get your bag and come width us."

"Yeah, Dad, she's in labor, I think. Looks like she peed herself, I told these two to find you so I could stay with her, but they were fascinated with her hair, which looks like a rainbow."

Before any of them can move, I'm running back to the meditation room to find Taz on the floor curled up on herself. Oh, fucking shit.

"Taz, hey, I'm here. Taz, look at me. RAQUEL, look at me, please."

"As usual, you can never handle a delicate situation. Rebel, my water broke, and my contractions are like three to four minutes apart. I think the baby is coming now."

Hearing noise behind me, I see first the three kids: one older and two younger, all boys. Then Mr. Macho gently moves them to the side and walks in, kneeling next to Taz.

"Oh no, get the hell outta of here, mister. We don't need you here. You want to be useful call nine-one-one for an ambulance. Otherwise, get gone now."

His head lifts and, believe it or not, he winks at me. Then I hear the older boy start talking as he moves closer to us after he motions for the little ones to stay by the door.

"Lady, you should be glad my dad's here. He's a doctor, no, he's an obstetrician, which is a doctor for women and babies. Let him help your friend, he knows what he's doing. Dad, I'll take these two out front, maybe go to the kid's room and let them play. I'll call nine-one-one too."

Just as he walks out, Taz lets out a wail like nothing I've ever heard before. I look down to see she's biting her lip, which is starting to bleed pretty bad. Fuck. Then Mr. Macho stands then leans down and picks—yeah, picks—Taz up, and is getting ready to place her on the massage table as we both hear a herd of cattle running down the hall. First in is Enforcer, and when he sees his wife not only in pain but also in the arms of a stranger, his face instantly goes blank, which is not a good thing. I'm sure he's thinking about when Raven had her shit that started in my gym.

"Hey, brother, he's a doctor or something. She's close, Enforcer, so please don't upset her. Go to her."

I watch as the dude gently lays Taz down and Enforcer goes to the other side, grabbing her hand and using his other hand to push her sweaty hair back. Half my club sisters are trying to squeeze into this average-size room, so I start shouting orders.

"Need someone to get some water. Another, some sheets and towels from the storage room. Shadow, you can stand the sight of blood, go help him. I doubt Enforcer is going to be any help. Peanut and Kitty, go check on this man's kids, think they're in the front room. Give them some juice boxes and snacks."

At that the doctor guy turns around to look at us.

"No juice for the older boy. He's diabetic, Type 1, so maybe water or even a sports water. I'd appreciate it."

The smile that appears on his face has every one of my sisters, and if I admit it, even me, taking a breath then letting out a sigh. His eyes twinkle like he knows the effect he has on women, but those eyes are locked on me.

Again, Taz begins wailing and shit, I don't know his name, so I ask.

"Hey, Doc, what's your name?"

Turning, he looks at me and grins.

"If you promise not to laugh, badass, I'll tell you."

As I nod, he's checking Taz's pulse and asking Enforcer some questions quietly.

"My name is Atlas Gianopoulos. And you are?"

"Motherfucker, we ain't on some goddamn dating game show. Take care of my wife if you want to continue breathing. Rebel, where the hell is that ambulance?"

Taz reaches up and caresses Enforcer's face.

"Travis, honey, it'll be good. Can you grab my bag

and place my crystals around the room? Give my sage to one of the sisters so she can smudge this room. Hurry, this little one is going to make their appearance soon."

"I'm not leaving your side, Que. Tink, Glory, you heard her, grab that bag and place her rocks around the room. Heartbreaker, can you get the dried weeds and blow smoke around the room, please?"

Taz giggles at his attempt to do what she wants. I hear Atlas tell Enforcer they need to get her undressed and Enforcer loses his mind. The doc never flinches, just calmly explains that for him to help deliver the baby she can't be wearing yoga pants and drawers. Taz is giggling so hard she passes wind. The room empties pretty quickly, except for Doc Atlas, Enforcer, Shadow, Tink, Glory, and me. Taz's face is as red as an apple, but Atlas just keeps explaining the ABCs of labor and delivery to Enforcer. Finally, he agrees and very carefully the two men slowly remove Taz's clothes. I just saw her the other day when I helped her take a shower but, man, her belly seems even bigger than that day, though now it's really dropped down. It is huge when they get her to move to remove her yoga pants, undies, and socks. Once she's naked from the waist down, Atlas puts her feet flat on the table and he flips the privacy blanket on top of her tummy so he can see underneath to examine her.

"Well, Miss Taz, you're right, this little one is on their way. Don't push until I tell you to. Can someone get me a clean sheet, preferably white? Also, that tray in the corner, push it next to the bed. Enforcer, before we get too involved, pull that T-shirt off of her. Bra too. Once the baby comes, we will need to put the child on her belly and chest. On second thought, take your shirt off too. No, don't argue, man, just do it. You'll thank me later."

Watching Atlas, you can tell the man knows exactly what he's doing. The confidence he has in himself is pretty sexy. So is every movement and his whispered words to Taz trying to keep her calm. The room now has crystals all over on the counters, floor, and even on the table she's lying on. Enforcer will do whatever she wants.

"Doctor, do we have time before the baby arrives for my sisters to set up the water bath so I can deliver the little one in there? I've researched it, and they say it's a better experience for the baby."

Before Atlas can even respond, Enforcer loses it.

"Que, goddamn it, told you that shit ain't gonna happen. Not having my kid drown before it takes its first breath. Let that shit go, please. I let you have the rocks and that smelly shit blown all over, let's be happy with that, woman."

I know it's coming, but damn, when it does, we all watch with our mouths open wide. With tears running down her face, Taz looks at her ol' man and lets loose. I'm totally shocked, as all my sisters are.

"Travis, get the hell out of here. I don't want your negative energy around me or my baby. Yeah, you donated the sperm but that's it. I've been growing and nurturing this child for nine months, so I should be able to decide how it makes its journey out into this fucked-up world we live in. My job as this baby's mother is to protect it, even from you if I have too. I said get out, until you can keep your energy down. Right now, I don't want to see you or have you in here. Please go."

Enforcer's mouth is open, eyes huge. Taz is now sobbing, trying to hide her face. He leans down, grabbing her hands and again shocks the shit outta all of us in the room.

"Que, shit, I'm so sorry. Please, Raquel, don't cry. You don't want our baby being born with you having sad energy. I'll personally go get that tub. Doc, what type of water should be in it?"

"Enforcer, usually lukewarm, not too cold or hot. If that's the plan, I suggest you move your ass. This baby isn't going to wait too long. Taz is dilated to just about eight centimeters, so I'd get moving."

At that moment more boots are hitting the floor as the rest of the Intruders make their presence known. Tank is the first in, followed by Yoggie with a huge black bag. Yeah, always a medic.

In no time at all, between the Intruders and Devil's Handmaidens, the tub is cleaned and almost filled by the assembly line Duchess started. The room is now almost empty. Atlas said he wanted it to be calm for Taz, so it's just Enforcer, Tink, Shadow, and me. Glory stepped out when she got a call from Momma Diane.

Shadow and I help Taz off the bed after we lowered it as far down as we could. Next, between all of us, we get her into the tub. She smiles when she's sitting in there looking at Enforcer.

"Come on, Travis, you know what I want."

He looks around at us with a scowl.

"If any of you say a word, I'll kill you with my own two hands, swear to Christ.

Then he takes his kutte off, placing it on one of the robe hooks, and then empties his pockets. Boots and socks are next. With his T-shirt already off, by the time his jeans hit the table Taz is panting through another contraction. Atlas is reaching in, trying to gauge how far along she is.

"Is there someone here who has some medical background? How about that man who brought in the bag? I could use a hand, no actually two."

Tink walks to the door and yells for Yoggie. When he walks to the door, she tells him he's needed.

Time seems to go quickly by as each contraction gets closer and closer. Enforcer is now behind Taz in the tub, holding her up. Atlas is scrunched down at the other end of the tub, doing what baby doctors do, I guess. He took his socks and gym shoes off. He was already in workout shorts, showing off his muscular calves. No, I didn't just think that. Yoggie is on the outside of the pool, right across from the doctor.

"Rebel, come here, I need you close."

Shit, just what I need, never done anything like this before. When I walk toward the tub, Enforcer smirks, so I flip him off.

"Keep it up, Dad, and you'll be sorry. Shadow, snap a picture of the Intruder's Enforcer in his boxers."

Just as Shadow snaps the pic, Taz screams and squeezes my hand so tight I think she might break it.

"That's it, Taz, doing great. Breathe, in and out. Come on, follow me. Take a deep breath, hold it for five, four, three, two, and one, release. Again, take your time and hold. Okay, we are there, so on the next contraction I need you to push as hard as you can."

We all wait for maybe thirty seconds when she lifts up a bit and bears down, moaning the whole time. Travis is holding her up and I'm letting her break one hand as the other is pushing her hair out of her face. When she leans back, I see Atlas and Yoggie looking at each other.

"What? Is there a problem? Come on, tell us so we can fix it, and let this little one celebrate their birth day."

"I think the cord is around the baby's neck, so just want Yoggie to be ready when the baby arrives. That's it, Auntie Rebel, so calm down. Shit, I mean, here we go. This time when she starts to push, Enforcer, lean down, push her forward so she bends more, which will help with pressure so the baby comes out. Everyone, get ready."

In my entire life I've never experienced anything like this. Taz breathing hard, face red, body tight, muscles all popping. Enforcer sweating as he helps Taz push their child out. Shadow is on the other side of Atlas, helping Yoggie out. Tink is the only one standing back and I know why. This has to hurt because she and Noodles have been trying to have their own baby. Damn it.

I hear Atlas yelling so I look down and can't believe

it. The baby is half in and half out. Yoggie is pulling the cord off its neck, and Shadow is holding one shoulder. Meanwhile, Atlas rotates the baby one way then the other until the other shoulder literally pops out. In less than a second Atlas has the baby out, and instead of a crack on its tiny wrinkly ass, he's rubbing up and down its back. Then he looks to the parents and smiles.

"Congratulations. It's a baby girl. Dad, want to cut the cord?"

Enforcer looks at Atlas then me and shakes his head.

"Let Rebel do it. I'm good where I'm at."

Atlas gives me what looks to be some sort of scissors and shows me where to cut between some clamps. When I do, I feel them rolling down my face. Shit. When I look up, Shadow and Tink are wiping their faces.

"What's her name, Mom and Dad?"

Taz and Enforcer both look to Atlas for a second then she leans back, whispering in his ear. They look at each other and kiss first then look back to Atlas.

"Doc, her name is Michelle, but we're going to call her Mickie."

My mouth falls open as my eyes fill even more. No way, they're naming their baby girl after me.

"Rebel, didn't think taking your club name was right, so Travis and I talked and this is what we came up with. Hope you don't mind?"

I shake my head as I have no words. When Atlas gets done cleaning the baby and doing whatever he does, then he shows Enforcer why his shirt is off. This is after Taz has gotten out of the water and so did her ol' man.

Atlas gives Mickie to her daddy, who then brings her on his bare chest. The look on his face is beyond priceless and when I look, Shadow is snapping pics. She looks my way and grins. Yeah, this is truly a once in a lifetime moment.

Finally, we hear the sirens and not too long after paramedics come running down the hall apologizing, saying they were stuck in traffic due to an accident shutting down the highway. Everyone in the hallway is waiting on news. No one says a word until Enforcer in his boxers leans out into the hallway and screams loudly for all to hear.

"It's a fuckin' baby girl. Our princess, Mickie, has arrived."

Seems like the paramedics know Atlas, well, at least the female one does. Once Taz and Mickie are all bundled up on the gurney, they wheel her out as everyone cheers. I look at the bloody water and the shit on the outside on the floor. Damn, I feel dizzy for some reason. What the fuck?

"Sit down, Rebel. Adrenaline can drop pretty fast. Hey, can someone grab me a bottle of water?"

I hear the little feet running down the hall. Atlas moves quickly to the doorway.

"Hey, guys, give me a few minutes then we can go. I'll take you for ice cream if you wait and be good. We got a deal?"

They nod and the little ones run back to the kid's room while the older one looks at his dad.

"All good, Dad?"

"Yeah, Son, she had a baby girl."

The kid smiles then turns and leaves. Atlas turns back to me with a bottle of water in his hands.

"Drink all of this. Now to even up. I did you a favor helping your friend out, so when do you want to go to dinner?"

I look at him like he has two heads. What the fuck is he talking about? So I ask. He smiles that sexy as shit smile my way. Bet he's gotten a lot of women with that one.

"Don't remember our deal? I help and you go to dinner with me. Can't back out now. I'll give you a day or two, but we are going to dinner, Rebel, or should I call you, Michelle?"

I feel nauseated when he says that name. No one, and I mean not a single soul, calls me that anymore. If anything, I go by Mya. I've even changed it legally.

"Atlas, don't ever call me that name again. And as grateful as I am for what you did for Taz, ain't no way in hell I'm going to dinner with someone who's head won't fit through any of the restaurants' doors in town. It's just too damn big."

He throws his head back and laughs. Then his eyes get serious when he leans close.

"We'll see, Rebel. Something you should know about me is, I always get what I want. See ya around, Feisty Rebel.

I watch him leave as a weird feeling takes shape in my stomach. I've come too far to fall for another good-looking, sexy guy who's full of himself. That ain't ever happening again. Though I did feel my nipples harden and my girlie garden start to tingle. Fuck it, not happening, no matter how gorgeous his eyes are. He's a dad of three boys and shit he could be married or have a partner. Besides I'm good by myself. I've got my club and sisters, which is all I need right now, or I try to convince myself as I get busy finishing cleaning up everything so I can go see my goddaughter. *Mickie is probably the closest thing I'll ever come to my own child* is my thought as I pick up all the soiled towels and sheets.

ABOUT THE AUTHOR

USA Today Bestselling author, D. M. Earl creates authentic and genuine characters while spinning stories that feel so real and relatable that the readers plunge deep within the plot, begging for more. Complete with drama, angst, romance, and passion, the stories jump off the page.

When Earl, an avid reader since childhood, isn't at her keyboard pouring her heart into her work, you'll find her in Northwest Indiana snuggling up to her husband, the love of her life, with her seven fur babies nearby. Her other passions include gardening and shockingly cruising around town on the back of her 2004 Harley. She's a woman of many talents and interests. Earl appreciates each and every reader who has ever given her a chance--and hopes to connect on social media with all of her readers.

Contact D.M at DM@DMEARL.COM
Website: http://www.dmearl.com/

- facebook.com/DMEarlAuthorIndie
- x.com/dmearl
- instagram.com/dmearl14
- amazon.com/D-M-Earl/e/B00M2HB12U
- bookbub.com/authors/d-m-earl
- goodreads.com/dmearl
- pinterest.com/dauthor

ALSO BY D.M. EARL

BLUE SKY SANCTUARY

Ollie's Recovery

Grey's Rescue

DEVIL'S HANDMAIDENS MC SPINOFF

Running Wild

Running Alone

DEVIL'S HANDMAIDENS MC: TIMBER-GHOST, MONTANA CHAPTER

Tink (Book #1)

Shadow (Book #2)

Taz (Book #3)

Vixen (Book #4)

Glory (Book #5)

Raven (Book #6)

Wildcat (Book #7)

Rebel (Book #8)

SUSAN STOKER'S OPERATION ALPHA (POLICE & FIRE)

Claire's Guardian

Lourde's Sentinel

GRIMM WOLVES MC SERIES

Behemoth (Book 1)

Bottom of the Chains-Prospect (Book 2)

Santa...Nope The Grimm Wolves (Book 3)

Keeping Secrets-Prospect (Book 4)

A Tormented Man's Soul: Part One (Book 5)

Triad Resumption: Part Two (Book 6)

Fractured Hearts - Prospect (Book 7)

WHEELS & HOGS SERIES

Connelly's Horde (Book 1)

Cadence Reflection (Book 2)

Gabriel's Treasure (Book 3)

Holidays with the Horde (Book 4)

My Sugar (Book 5)

Daisy's Darkness (Book 6)

THE JOURNALS TRILOGY

Anguish (Book 1)

Vengeance (Book 2)

Awakening (Book 3)

Printed in Great Britain
by Amazon